THE
GOLD TRAIN
BANDITS

AN
AMERICAN ADVENTURE
SERIES

THE GOLD TRAIN BANDITS

LEE RODDY

BETHANY HOUSE PUBLISHERS
MINNEAPOLIS, MINNESOTA 55438

01019 1368

Published in association with the literary
agency of Alive Communications, P.O. Box
49068, Colorado Springs, Colorado 80949

Published by Bethany House Publishers
A Ministry of Bethany Fellowship, Inc.
6820 Auto Club Road, Minneapolis, Minnesota 55438

Printed in the United States of America

Library of Congress Cataloging-in-Publication Data

Roddy, Lee, 1921–
    The gold train bandits / Lee Roddy.
       p. cm. — (An American adventure ; bk. 8)
    Summary: Twelve-year-old Hildy and her family have a hard life in
California during the Depression, but her efforts to help the daughter of
an outlaw strengthens Hildy's faith.

    [1. Robbers and outlaws—Fiction. 2. Depressions—1929—Fiction.
3. Christian life—Fiction.] I. Title. II. Series: Roddy, Lee, 1921–
American adventure ; bk. 8.
PZ7.R6Go   1992
[Fic]—dc20   92–5045
ISBN 1–55661–211–7   CIP
                                            AC

To
Etta Jagger,
a special friend
1925–1992

LEE RODDY is a bestselling author and motivational speaker. Many of his more than 50 books, such as *Grizzly Adams*, *Jesus*, *The Lincoln Conspiracy*, the *D. J. Dillon Adventure Series*, and the *Ladd Family Adventures* have been bestsellers, television programs, book club selections or have received special recognition. All of his books support traditional moral, spiritual, and family values.

CONTENTS

MYSTERY AT THE ABANDONED HOUSE

Monday Afternoon

Hildy Corrigan suddenly broke off her happy humming when she heard heavy footsteps coming toward her from inside the scary old house. She paused, right hand poised to knock again on the front door when she saw the white porcelain knob slowly turning.

A khaki-colored army overcoat draped over the frosted oval window swayed slightly as the door opened about an inch on its creaking, rusty hinges. Through the crack, the twelve-year-old girl could see the stubble of a black beard on a man's cheek. A lock of greasy dark hair fell over one brown eye.

"Yeah?" the man growled through the crack.

Startled at the unfriendly voice, the blue-eyed girl took a half-step back. She almost tripped over a bicycle leaning against the square pillar.

"Uh—" she began uncertainly, "I'm your neighbor. My family and I live across the field." She pointed toward a tar-paper shack half a mile away. "I saw a girl here about my age. Since this old house has been empty so long, and there are no other neighbors closer than a mile, I thought maybe she'd like to—"

"Ain't no girl here." The voice was cold and hard.

"Oh, but I saw her!" Hildy cried without thinking. "Twice! Yesterday she was helping put coverings over the windows. A few minutes ago when I got off the bus—"

"I told you, they ain't no girl here!" the man interrupted.

Hildy glanced at the bicycle. She wanted to point to it and say, *That's a girl's bike*, but she kept silent.

The man seemed to read her mind. He snapped, "That's mine!"

Hildy told herself it couldn't be so, but she stood uncertainly for a moment, unable to understand the man's denial.

He interrupted her thoughts. "I told you they ain't no girl here. Go 'way! Don't come back, or you'll be sorry!"

He slammed the door so hard the makeshift covering slipped off to one side. Instantly, the man grabbed it in an effort to put it in place again. But not before Hildy had a glimpse inside the house.

A shaft of early November sunlight showed three men standing near the door. Each held a gun.

Alarmed, Hildy's heart sped up. She turned around so rapidly that one of her long brunette braids flopped against the bicycle. Her eyes focused on it. *I know I saw her riding this!* she thought, *So why'd that man lie to me? And why are those men inside carrying guns?*

Her thoughts were interrupted by a man's angry voice from inside the house. This was followed by what sounded like a slap and a cry of pain.

For a moment, Hildy hesitated, unsure what to do. Her heartbeat increased again as a sense of danger crept over her.

What's going on? she wondered. *Maybe I'd better get home and tell Molly.*

Hildy started walking down the long dirt lane with stubble from the wheat fields on both sides. She sensed hostile eyes boring into her back. She was also keenly aware of just how barren and lonely it was in this remote area of rolling brown hills.

After about a couple hundred yards, Hildy reached the top of a small hill. She stopped and glanced back.

There was something spooky about the two-story house. It stood forlornly on a desolate, treeless knoll above the wheat fields. They had been harvested, leaving only the dry yellow stubble on all four sides. The box-like frame house had apparently been built well before the turn of the century. The elements had long ago beaten the structure into a drab, weathered gray.

About seventy-five yards behind the house, a California hip-style barn leaned precariously to the left. A week ago, Hildy and her cousin, Ruby Konning, had explored the barn through sliding doors that had been left open. Then the girls had approached the house, where Hildy commented that the dirty windows seemed to stare like dead but open eyes.

Inside, Hildy and Ruby had found only old newspapers scattered about the bare first floor. The sagging stairs to the second-story bedrooms had creaked and groaned at the girls' intrusion. It was a scary experience, so the cousins hurriedly left the old house.

Looking at it now, Hildy could see no more signs of life than she and Ruby had found, except for the makeshift coverings over the windows and the closed barn door. Hildy wondered what secrets they hid.

I've got to know what's going on back there, she told herself. *There's something wrong, and that girl might be in trouble. If she is, I've got to help her.*

Still feeling a sense of danger, Hildy broke into a run. She didn't stop until she reached her home, a small frame tar-paper shack rented for $15 a month. Rolls of black roofing paper covered the outside walls and roof. The economic depression that had begun in 1929 seemed to be worse now, five years later.

The ugly shack was a step up from where Hildy had lived in the past. Born in a sharecropper's cabin, she had often moved with her family as her father sought work. The Corrigans had never had an indoor bathroom, electric lights, or even a battery-operated radio. When they arrived in California last summer, they first lived in a tent along the river. Next they moved to a barn, then to this tar-paper shack.

Hildy hated moving, always leaving friends and relatives behind, changing schools, never having permanent roots. Shortly after her mother died nearly nineteen months ago, after giving birth to Joey, and their father was off somewhere looking for work, Hildy had comforted her four younger sisters with a promise:

"Our daddy'll come back and take us off someplace where we'll never have to move again. There'll be no more sharecroppers' cabins or tumbledown shacks in the Ozarks. In California, we'll find a nice big house where we'll be together always. It'll be our 'forever' home."

It was this heart's desire that kept Hildy's eyes on the brighter future, so she accepted the tar-paper shack as a step toward fulfilling her vision. She crossed the front porch, one side of which had been closed off to make an extra bedroom for her three younger sisters.

She called, "Hi, everybody. I'm home."

Molly, her stepmother, answered. "I'm in our bedroom changing Joey. Sarah and Iola are playing out back. Elizabeth and Martha aren't home from school yet."

Hildy's pet raccoon came waddling toward her from the living room, chirring in greeting. "Hello, Mischief," Hildy said. She picked up her pet and settled it on the back of her neck. The masked animal's hind legs hung down on either side of Hildy's neck, and its forepaws gripped the base of her braids.

Hildy hurried past the converted bedroom on her left, the one that was originally part of the front porch, now boarded up except on the front. A clear waterproof covering over the rusted screen made little snapping noises as the rising wind passed. Hildy's sisters, Martha, Sarah and Iola, ages seven, five and three, had metal-frame beds here. Elizabeth, being ten, shared an inside bedroom with Hildy.

Hildy turned to her right and stopped in the doorway to her father and stepmother's bedroom. "Hi," she said.

Molly looked up from bending over the two-tone ivory and green enameled double bed where nineteen-month-old Joey lay. Molly had gentle brown eyes and dark hair with a few streaks of gray. She wasn't much taller than Hildy, but she was very strong. Molly finished pinning Joey's three-cornered diaper made of old cloths.

She glanced up at Hildy and smiled in greeting. "You're late. Did the bus break down again?"

"No." Hildy set Mischief on the floor, leaned over and lightly kissed her brother's forehead. "Hi, Joey," she said, grinning down at him. He looked at her with listless eyes. He could say several words, but now he didn't speak or even smile. "You okay?" she asked.

"He's been listless all day," Molly explained. "Woke up from his nap pulling at his right ear."

Hildy studied her brother a moment. "You have an earache, Joey?"

Molly explained, "I've heard that blowing smoke into a child's ear helps, but nobody in this family smokes. Besides, I think that's just an old wives' tale."

"He seems all right now," Hildy observed, and returned to Molly's earlier question. "I stopped at that old house where a new girl just moved in."

"What's she like?" Molly tugged the baby's faded hand-me-down shirt over his head, then stopped. She placed her palm on his abdomen and frowned. "Hildy, does he feel a little warm to you?"

Hildy touched her brother's forehead just as angry cries erupted from the backyard. "That's mine! Give it back!" This was answered by a vehement, "No, mine!"

Molly headed out of the bedroom. "Those girls! They're at it again!" As she hurried through the house toward the kitchen, she called over her shoulder, "Will you look after Joey?"

"Sure," Hildy replied, gently ruffling the baby's soft crown of pale hair. Like all his sisters except Hildy, he was going to be a towhead. Hildy moved her palm down to Joey's forehead and left it there a moment.

Wish we could afford a thermometer, she thought. *Maybe he just feels warm from being indoors.* "Come on, Joey," she said. "I want to tell Molly what happened at the neighbors'."

Joey lifted his little arms and said, "Up." Hildy picked him up, but he didn't smile as he usually did when she carried him. She kissed him quickly on top of his head and murmured, "I love you, Joey."

Hildy carried him into the living room. Mischief followed, complaining noisily about not being carried.

They crossed the faded linoleum, passing between a cane-bottom chair, an ancient hickory rocker, and a broken-down davenport. One of its springs stuck up from the cushion. Two small homemade pine tables completed the furniture in the room. One table held a purple glass vase; the other supported an open black-bound Bible. There was no radio or phonograph, not even books or newspapers.

Joey squirmed to be let down.

Hildy lowered him to the floor. He'd been walking since he was about a year old. He followed Hildy and Mischief through the door into the dining room with its homemade pine table and benches. A kerosene lamp with a smudge of smoke on the tall glass chimney rested on the oilcloth-covered table.

Hildy took one of Joey's small hands and stepped down into the lean-to kitchen. It had only one full wall on the south side where the heavy winter winds and rains would beat against it. The other sides had boards up about four feet. From there, wire screen extended almost to the ceiling. The screen was covered with a clear waterproof fabric that let in light but helped keep out the rain.

Molly came in from outside, and Hildy heard a snatch of conversation from the two little sisters, whose disagreement their stepmother had resolved. Now they played near the back door.

Molly said, "You were telling me about the new neighbor girl."

"You won't believe what happened," Hildy replied, opening the pantry door. The raccoon dashed inside and began playing like a kitten with its reflection in the side of a fifty-gallon lard can. Hildy picked up a small raw potato and the ring from a Mason jar lid. She handed them to Joey.

The family had no toys, but the little boy played with what he had. He plopped down on the faded linoleum and began trying to push the potato through the ring.

Hildy turned to Molly, who was starting to shake down the ashes in the wood-burning stove. Hildy briefly explained about her experience, including her glimpse of the armed men.

Molly didn't seem concerned. "The man at the door was probably rude to you because he was embarrassed, figuring his family wasn't ready for company yet."

"What about the men with the guns?"

"They could have been friends getting ready to go hunting. There are plenty of quail in the river bottom and pheasants in the open fields. You'd better change and start supper now."

Not feeling satisfied with Molly's answers, Hildy turned back to the second bedroom that opened off the dining room. She and ten-year-old Elizabeth slept on army cots here. It was far better than the pallets of old clothes, coats, and blankets they had at the barn-house where they'd lived until recently.

Hildy sat on the edge of a packing crate that served as both nightstand and chair. She removed her sturdy brown shoes and raised her voice. "I didn't like it, Molly. There was something scary about it."

"I'm sure there's a logical explanation," Molly said.

Hildy wasn't so sure. She absently took off her green-and-white print skirt, which hung just below her knees. Her knees showed the scars she'd gotten from picking cotton when she was only five.

"When Ruby comes by, maybe she'll go with me so we can watch for that girl again," Hildy said, sliding the skirt onto a wooden hanger and placing it on a large nail in the wall.

"Since the man warned you not to come back, you and your cousin had better stay away," Molly said, sounding a bit uneasy. "At least, until your father gets home and we can talk to him about it."

Wearing her faded blue-and-white checked housedress, Hildy started for the kitchen, then stopped, listening. "Sounds like Brother Ben's car," she told her stepmother.

Hildy picked up Joey and followed Molly through the house and onto the front steps. They watched as Ben Strong, former U.S. Marshal and Texas Ranger, eased his 1929 Packard 645 Victoria up the rutted driveway. The canvas top was offset by bright yellow body paint and brown trim, white sidewall tires, glistening chrome radiator, hood ornament, and triple headlights.

"Howdy," the eighty-six-year-old gentleman said with a friendly smile. He gave his white walrus moustache a flip with the back of his right forefinger and stepped out onto the running board. He reached back into the front seat and recovered his white Stetson hat. He held it in one hand, standing straight and tall in his highly polished tan cowboy boots.

Hildy and Molly returned the greeting and invited their guest inside. As they entered the living room, Hildy commented, "I thought you were up in the foothills, trying to catch those bandits who are supposed to be planning to rob the gold train."

"I was." The old ranger had a soft drawl. "But the fact is, we don't know for sure that there's going to be a robbery attempt. So far, all we have are rumors."

"Is that why you're back down here in the valley?" Hildy asked, motioning for Ben to take a seat.

He sank onto the couch, crossed his long legs, and hooked the Stetson over the toe of his boot. He looked very distinguished with his full head of white hair.

Hildy sat down on an old cane-bottom chair with Joey on her lap. Molly eased into the rocker in an obvious effort to keep it from squeaking. She didn't succeed too well, as Ben continued his explanation.

"The police contacts who hired me to help stop this rumored gold train robbery say it looks like the Hux Stonecipher gang is involved."

"Huxley Stonecipher? I've heard of him!" Hildy exclaimed as Joey stopped clutching to her and looked at the visitor with lessening shyness. "Bank robber, isn't he?"

Molly shuddered. "Cold-blooded killer too. Four, five murders so far, I heard."

"He and his gang are suspected of half a dozen," the ex-lawman agreed somberly, "but Stonecipher's never been caught. Since the FBI got John Dillinger last July, Stonecipher's probably the most notorious outlaw left in the whole country."

"Do you think his gang's planning to rob the train, Brother Ben?" Hildy asked.

"If it is, it'll be a first for him. He's always stuck to banks so far. Law-enforcement officers are hoping to get a lead on him through his daughter."

"His daughter?" Hildy asked.

Ben nodded. "Yup. She's about your age, Hildy. She was kidnapped from her mother about ten days ago. Mrs. Stonecipher divorced Hux after he turned bad, but she naturally got custody of the girl. They moved from their original home in Oklahoma to somewhere in New York state.

"Authorities believe Stonecipher found them and abducted his own daughter—maybe just to spite his ex-wife. Now authorities are looking for him and the girl. When they catch him, every banker in the West can rest easy again. So can regular folks."

Molly sighed. "I feel sorry for his daughter. It must be hard, having an outlaw for a father."

"The worst part," Ben said, "is that she'll always have to hide out and keep moving from place to—" He broke off suddenly. "What's the matter with Joey?"

Hildy looked down in alarm at her little brother in her lap.

His arms were jerking stiffly up and down.

"Joey!" Hildy cried out just as his head fell against her.

Joey's eyes rolled back so that only the whites showed. Then he went completely limp.

Chapter Two

A SUDDEN THOUGHT

Late Monday Afternoon

Joey!" Hildy cried, looking down at her little brother's limp body. "What's wrong?"

There was no answer from the small child.

Molly gently but firmly took the boy. "He's burning up with fever!" she exclaimed. "Quick, Hildy! Get some cold water and towels. Hurry!"

Hildy scrambled to comply as Molly rushed into her bedroom with the toddler. Brother Ben followed close behind, leaving his big white hat on the floor.

"Oh, Lord! Please don't let anything happen to Joey!" Hildy prayed as she darted into the kitchen. She jerked open a door below the sink and wildly yanked out old flour sacks that served as dish towels.

The raccoon hurried out of the pantry with her usual rolling gait and stood up on hind legs, wanting to be picked up. Hildy groaned, "Not now, Mischief!" She lifted the coon gently, opened the back door and set her on the step. The animal protested noisily as Hildy closed the door and turned back to the sink.

She quickly soaked the cloths under the faucet, then ran with them, dripping wet, into the bedroom. She rushed past the old ranger, who stood at the foot of the bed, and held out the towels to her stepmother, who was bent over the still, small form, now shirtless.

"What is it, Molly?" Hildy asked anxiously.

"I don't know." Her stepmother applied one towel to Joey's forehead, letting little rivulets of water run down his cheeks and into the bed. "I've never seen a fever come up so fast." She wrapped the other towels around the baby's face, neck, chest, and abdomen.

Ben asked softly, "Shall we take him to the doctor?"

Molly didn't look up but adjusted the cloths, starting at the forehead. "We can't afford a doctor."

Hildy knew that was true, and that her father didn't really believe in doctors, anyway. But she had to protest in alarm, "We can't let Joey die!"

"He won't die!" Molly said brusquely.

Ben replied, "I'll take care of the doctor's bill."

Molly's voice softened, "I can't let you do that, Ben. But thanks anyway."

Joey's eyes flickered open.

Hildy exclaimed, "He's coming out of it!"

The little boy looked blankly around the room, his blue eyes resting first on his stepmother, then his sister, and finally on the old ranger.

Hildy leaned close to him. "Are you all right, Joey?" she asked anxiously, stroking the top of his head. He looked up with eyes that didn't seem to recognize her. He lay still, not making a sound.

Molly picked him up, the wet cloths instantly making dark spots on her dress. "I'll hold him awhile," she said, stepping past Hildy and into the living room. "You'll need to get some more wet cloths so we can replace these as they get warm."

Hildy nodded and ran into the kitchen as the back door opened. Five-year-old Martha and three-year-old Iola entered.

Their hands and faces were smudged, and their dresses dirty. Even their blonde, almost white hair, was peppered with dirt.

"Stand right there!" Hildy instructed firmly. "I'll be right back to help you get cleaned up, soon as I take these cloths to Joey."

"What's the matter with him?" Martha asked, apparently sensing her older sister's concern.

Iola was less discerning. "I'm hungry," she said.

"There are some cold boiled potatoes on the windowsill," Hildy said, heading toward the living room. "But don't touch them until your hands are washed!"

When Hildy entered the living room, Molly stopped rocking in the squeaking old chair. Joey was restless, trying to take off the damp cloths.

Molly said, "I think he's going to be all right, but we've got to keep the fever coming down. Hildy, you put the rags on him while I hold his hands. Otherwise, he'll throw them off."

It took some quiet but firm talk from Hildy to get the little boy to leave the cold cloths in place. When she reached out to adjust the one on his forehead, she blinked in surprise. "He's almost back to normal."

Molly placed a hand near Hildy's. "You're right. Thank God!" Then she removed the cloth from Joey's abdomen and nodded. "Even allowing for the coolness from the cloth, I'm sure his fever's going down pretty fast."

The old ranger cleared his throat. "You sure you don't want me to take him to the doctor? There'd be no cost to you."

"No, thanks. I'm sure he's going to be just fine."

"Then if you won't need me, I'll be going," Ben announced, rising.

"But you didn't say why you came," Molly protested.

"It'll keep," the old ranger said in his soft drawl. "Uh—Molly, would you walk out to the car with me?"

Hildy shot a puzzled look at the ranger. He wouldn't meet her eyes, which gave her an uneasy feeling.

"Why, sure," Molly said, standing up with the baby. "Hildy,

would you hold Joey until I—" She broke off as Sarah let out a shriek from the kitchen.

"I'll take care of them," Hildy said, taking the baby from her stepmother. "You go on with Brother Ben."

Hildy quickly said goodbye to the old ranger, then carried Joey into the kitchen, with Sarah leading the way. Hildy was concerned because Ben obviously had something he didn't want to say in front of her. But she forgot that when she entered the kitchen and saw Iola.

The little girl had taken the white granite pan of boiled potatoes from the windowsill where they'd been set to keep cool. The Corrigans had no icebox. Even if they had, there were no deliveries of ice to this remote part of the county. The potatoes were all over the floor, mashed under the bare feet of the three-year-old.

"Smashing potatoes," the child announced with a happy smile. She stamped down hard on another one.

Holding on to Joey, who seemed to feel better by the minute, Hildy spoke firmly. "Iola, you can't do that! Food isn't to play with. Daddy works hard to get enough money to buy potatoes. They cost ninety-eight cents for a hundred-pound sack, and Daddy earns only two-and-a-half dollars a day. If you waste these, we could all go hungry."

Iola said defensively, "Joey plays with potatoes."

"Yes," Hildy admitted, "but the ones he plays with are raw. When they're cooked, you can't play with them. Now, set those ruined potatoes outside for Mischief, but don't let her in. Then get a washrag and I'll clean you up."

Hildy heard the Packard's big motor start as she finished washing Iola's face, hands, and feet. Moments later, Molly stepped down into the kitchen. Her face was so somber that Hildy became worried.

"What's the matter?" she cried, standing up and shifting Joey to her right hip.

Molly didn't answer Hildy, but instead spoke to the little sisters. "You two go outside and play."

"We already played outside," Sarah protested.

"Then go watch for Elizabeth and Martha. They should be coming home from school about now." Molly gently but firmly pushed the girls out of the kitchen.

"What is it?" Hildy asked as her stepmother turned to face her. "What did Brother Ben say?"

Molly didn't answer until she'd felt Joey's forehead, then his abdomen. "The fever's gone," she announced quietly, then added, "Ben said he's seen something like it a few times before. He says some little kids get middle-ear infections, but they usually outgrow them."

"Usually? What happens if they don't?"

"Well, sometimes it's necessary for a doctor to lance the area to drain the infection."

"You mean, an operation?"

"Ben says it's not exactly an operation."

"But we don't have money for anything like that."

"I know." Molly absently pulled a flour sack from a nail and wrapped it around her waist to serve as an apron. "This will probably be the only time Joey is bothered by it, and he'll be all right."

Hildy's little brother was back on the floor trying to push a raw potato through a Mason jar ring. His cheek was cool to the touch, no more sign of fever. Joey looked up and grinned at Hildy, as if he'd never been sick a day in his life.

Hildy straightened up and asked her stepmother, "But what'll happen if Joey has another spell, and he can't have the operation?"

Molly took another deep breath. "Ben reminded me he's not a doctor, but he's seen a couple of cases where mastoiditis developed. That has something to do with a bone behind the ear getting inflamed."

"What happens then?" Hildy prompted.

Molly turned back to the stove. "That's not going to happen to Joey. He's going to be all right."

Hildy had an uneasy feeling. Her stepmother was being evasive. "Is there something you're not telling me?"

Molly lifted a lid from a pan on the stove, then stopped and looked somberly into Hildy's eyes. "If that happens, Ben says Joey could die."

Hildy swallowed hard. She knew about death. She still ached from the death of her mother when Joey was born. And Molly had lost her first husband, and then her only child. The possibility of something happening to her only brother frightened Hildy terribly.

She forced the thought away and tried to think about the new girl next door, but Hildy's mind wouldn't stay focused. She bustled about the kitchen, washing and drying breakfast and lunch dishes.

When Elizabeth and Martha got home from school, they changed clothes and came to the kitchen where Hildy was starting to make biscuits.

Seven-year-old Martha groaned, "Not biscuits again! Why can't we have bread from the store?"

"Because it costs money," Elizabeth replied, "and we don't have any. That's why!"

"When Daddy took us to town last Saturday, the store had a pound loaf for only nine cents," Martha protested.

Hildy explained, "But Daddy can buy forty-nine pounds of flour for just a dollar and fifty-five cents. We not only make our own bread, biscuits, and rolls, but we can sew the empty sacks into underclothes. Every penny counts in these hard times."

Elizabeth added, "You're too little to remember, Martha, but Mother never did buy bread from a store. Isn't that right?"

Hildy nodded. "She used to say she felt sorry for any woman who had to buy store bread. She had to be a mighty sorry cook if she couldn't make her own family biscuits or rolls."

At the mention of their mother, all three girls fell silent. Hildy's thoughts returned to her little brother's possible danger, but she again shook off the thought. She wondered why Brother Ben had come visiting, then left without saying why.

Darkness fell early in November, so shortly after five o'clock, Molly lit the coal-oil lamps.

Moments later, Sarah called from the front door, "Car coming! And it's not Daddy."

Visitors to the remote Corrigan home were infrequent, so Hildy joined the rest of the family as they watched the headlights bouncing up the rutted dirt road. It didn't sound like Brother Ben's powerful Packard; more like a Model T Ford.

"It's Uncle Nate," Elizabeth announced.

Nate Konning was an uncle to the Corrigan children. That made his thirteen-year-old daughter, Ruby, their cousin—and Hildy's best friend.

A few minutes later the tall, slender man, wearing a hand-me-down brown suit, entered the living room, followed by his feisty only child. They carefully sat down on the couch, avoiding the spring that stuck up through the upholstery.

Like millions of other Americans at the time, Nate was unemployed. He'd been a cowboy, and even a hated sheepherder, but lately he'd felt a call to preach. He served no regular church, so he supported himself with part-time ranch work and occasional preaching.

"We got news fer y'all," Ruby began in her mountaineer accent. Hildy had noticed that her cousin seemed to take special delight in talking the way she had in her native Ozarks, which she had left last summer. Ruby was slightly taller than Hildy, with short blonde hair and hazel eyes. She wore her favorite tomboy clothes—a rumpled blue shirt and faded overalls.

"Now, Ruby," her father chided gently, "it's not polite for company to start right in talking until folks have said their *howdy-do's* and such."

Nate was a lanky widower in his mid-thirties. He lightly touched his blond hair that he wore parted in the middle and plastered down on both sides with a rose-fragrance oil. It made the hair glisten like patent leather shoes.

Ruby's rebellious nature erupted. "Nobody never said I was born polite!" she declared. Shifting on the sofa, she turned her bright hazel eyes on everyone. "Daddy's got hisself called to a reg'lar church to preach in," she declared triumphantly. "Lone

River Bible Church. An' yo're all invited to come next Sunday and hear him."

Hildy and Molly both told Nate they were glad for him, and asked what time the services would be. Before Nate could answer, lights flashed as a car turned from the county road onto the Corrigans' long driveway.

"That's Daddy's Rickenbacker!" Hildy exclaimed, jumping up and going to the front door. She was afraid when she thought about what her father would say about Joey's possible need for surgery. Her father could be very stubborn sometimes, but maybe he wouldn't be when it involved his only son and namesake.

Joe Corrigan had a short temper, and the moment he entered the lamplight, Hildy saw that he was angry. His blue eyes glittered in contrast to his deeply tanned face. He wore ancient blue jeans and scuffed cowboy boots. When he pulled off his wide-brimmed sombrero, a pale white band of skin showed where the sweatband of his hat had been. His stubby black beard made his anger seem more threatening.

Without greeting anyone, he grumbled, "Some girl on a bike without any light almost caused me to wreck the car down the road a piece. I jumped out to blister her ears with some choice words, but she rode off real fast. What in thunderation was a girl Hildy's age doing out there after dark? And where does she live?"

In her concern over Joey, Hildy had forgotten about her strange experience at the old ranch house and something the old ranger had said. Suddenly those thoughts flashed back, and the words of her father clanged in Hildy's mind like a fire-alarm bell.

She glanced in the direction of the distant ranch house and whispered, "Outlaw's daughter!"

CHAPTER
THREE
——

HARD TIMES

Monday Night and Tuesday Morning

Hildy's father looked at her. "What do you mean 'outlaw's daughter'?"

Hildy knew it wouldn't be safe to discuss her ideas about the new neighbors in front of her younger sisters. They were certain to say something at school, and if Hildy was right, that could be dangerous.

She asked the four little girls to go into the kitchen and play with Mischief. They resisted, especially Elizabeth, who felt she was "big enough" and should be allowed to stay. But when their father spoke to them, all four obeyed.

When the kitchen door was shut, Hildy lowered her voice. She briefly told about seeing the new girl, the strange encounter with the mysterious man in the old ranch house, and the men she saw with guns. Then Hildy added the old ranger's news about the outlaw, Huxley Stonecipher, kidnapping his own daughter from her mother.

Hildy concluded, "So I think the girl you saw in the road is the same one I saw at that old house."

Joe Corrigan scowled in deep thought. "Are you saying you

think that she's the outlaw's daughter?"

Hildy hesitated, feeling a little foolish now at the idea. Perhaps it was unlikely, but she slowly nodded. "It could be."

Molly exclaimed, "My stars, Joe! If that's true, and those armed men next door are part of that gang, we could all be murdered in our beds!"

"Now hold your horses!" Joe replied, his voice softer than before. "We don't know that Hildy's right."

Nate asked quietly, "But what if she is?"

The adults began discussing the subject in anxious, whispered tones. Hildy and Ruby listened awhile, then eased away from the grown-ups. The cousins walked into the dining room, past the lighted kerosene lamp on the table, to the window.

They stared through it toward the distant ranch house. It was dark, but a faint, moving glow showed through cracks in the barn wall, as though someone were carrying a lantern.

Ruby asked, "Ye really reckon them's crooks over yonder?"

"I don't know what to think," Hildy admitted.

"What do ye reckon we should do?"

"Dad and Uncle Nate'll figure it out, so we don't have to think about it." Hildy turned and led the way back into the living room.

The adults explained that the mysterious neighbors had no reason to harm the Corrigans. And whoever they were, they had no reason to be concerned about a twelve-year-old girl trying to be friendly. The armed men probably wouldn't give another thought to Hildy's brief visit, especially if they were hunters, as Molly had suggested.

However, just to play it safe, Nate said he would drive over to Ben Strong's place and ask his opinion. As a former law-enforcement officer, Ben would have some good suggestions. He would also know what to do about quietly checking out the new neighbors without arousing suspicion or endangering the Corrigan family.

Nate reminded the Corrigans that they were invited to hear him at eleven o'clock next Sunday at the tiny Lone River Bible

Church. Hildy planned to be there. Molly said she would if she could, but Joe said nothing. He didn't hold much to spiritual matters.

When her cousin and uncle had gone to see the old ranger, Hildy had mixed feelings. She wanted very much to hear what her father would say about Joey going to the doctor, but before she or Molly could mention that, Joe spoke up.

"Hildy, you're old enough to know this," he began, his face solemn. "Molly, I was going to tell you first, after the kids were in bed, but I may as well say it now. I've been laid off."

"Oh, no!" Molly exclaimed.

"It's supposed to be only for a few days," he explained. "Things are quiet at the ranch, so the boss is letting most of the riders off."

"Without pay?" Molly guessed.

Her husband nodded. "But don't worry. I borrowed a spear from one of the men. While I'm off I'll go down to the river and try my luck. I should be able to get enough salmon to can or salt down so we'll have something to eat through the winter."

"Oh, Joe, not tonight!" his wife pleaded. "Those men next door—"

"Forget them, Molly!" Her husband looked at her with tired eyes that showed more concerns than being laid off. "We've decided that whoever they are, they have no reason to bother us. I wouldn't leave you or the kids if I wasn't sure of that. Besides, salmon are easier to spear at night. I'll get my flashlight and go right after supper. Now let's eat. I'm starved."

Hildy didn't sleep well that night. She a bad dream about a man with greasy dark hair and one eye chasing her as she rode on a girl's bike. She pedalled hard, but the man overtook her. He reached out, grabbed her shoulder, and started to yank her off the bike. She felt his rough, black beard on her cheek.

"Hildy, wake up!" It was Elizabeth's voice.

Hildy raised her head off the army cot. It was almost daylight. By the faint glow coming in their bedroom window, Hildy could see Mischief sleeping at the foot of her bed. Elizabeth stood on the bare wooden floor in her homemade nightgown.

"You were moaning and groaning so much I couldn't sleep," Elizabeth explained, "so I shook you."

Hildy sat up. Her long hair, unbraided, cascaded over her face. She brushed it away with her hands, and shoved the heavy handmade quilt aside just as her father knocked on the door.

"Girls, you up?"

"Yes, Daddy," they said in unison.

"Come see what grew on the apricot tree last night."

The girls looked at each other, not understanding their father's remark. Not having robes, they wrapped the quilts around their shoulders. The only source of heat in the house was the wood-burning stove in the kitchen. This was allowed to go out at night, and the morning air was downright cold.

Hildy was relieved that she'd been only dreaming about the one-eyed man. With Mischief riding her shoulders and hanging on to her locks of hair, she and Elizabeth entered the kitchen. The stove was just starting to put out a pleasant warmth.

Their father picked up a five-celled flashlight and opened the back door. "Take a look outside," he said.

As the sisters peered out, their father snapped on the light and focused it on the one lone tree in the backyard. The apricots had ripened in June and fallen off. A few pits lay on the bare ground. The leaves had recently fallen, but the branches sagged with something sleek and silvery.

"They're fish!" Hildy exclaimed, her breath making little puffs in the crisp predawn air.

"Salmon," Joe said, moving the light. Ten of them. Some weigh up to fifty pounds or more. See that one there?" The light steadied on a long body with an undershot jaw. "That one's nearly as long as you are."

Elizabeth asked, "Is spearing that many fish against the law, Daddy?"

He turned off the flashlight. "I took only the legal limit. As I was putting them into my car, the game warden came along. Name's MacKaffrey. We've known each other for a while. He said that he'd just confiscated five fish from another spearman who'd exceeded the limit.

"MacKaffrey had let the man go with a warning, but seized the extra fish. Since MacKaffrey knows I have a big family, he told me to take the extra salmon because they'd be wasted if he took them back to his office."

Hildy frowned, remembering something she'd heard her father quote about "fish in possession." If she understood that properly, the warden's motives might have been good. However, he had been wrong in giving the fish away because that left Hildy's father with more than the legal limit in his possession. Hildy wondered if her father had been wrong to even accept the extra salmon.

Even if Daddy is wrong, she told herself, *this is the only thing he thinks he can do to help keep his family from starving. I hope God will be merciful to him.* She changed the subject: "Daddy, did Molly talk to you about Joey?"

"Yes. He seems fine, but I'll take him in to see old Mrs. Radcliffe this morning. She knows a lot about nursing sick people and such things."

Hildy nodded, believing that the local practical nurse probably did know something about everything. She never charged anything, but grateful people always took her some of their own meager food as payment.

Hildy asked, "What if she says Joey needs an operation?"

"You girls both know we have no money for doctors." Her father's voice was sad, yet it sounded to Hildy as though he wanted her and Elizabeth to understand how much it hurt him to say that.

Elizabeth said, "Maybe you could borrow the money."

"Nobody'll loan me anything because I've got no collateral. There's nothing they can take if I can't repay a loan."

"Could you get a loan from Matthew Farnham?" Hildy asked.

She and Ruby sometimes worked part time for Mrs. Farnham, wife of Lone River's only banker. Mrs. Farnham had polio and was confined to a wheelchair. Hildy and Ruby did house-work and took care of the Farnhams' two small children.

"I couldn't ask him," Joe Corrigan said sadly. "He's my friend."

"All the better!" Elizabeth cried, clapping her hands. "He won't turn you down."

"You don't understand, girls. He wouldn't turn me down, but I can't repay him, so I won't ask. I'd never do that to any-body—especially Matt Farnham."

Hildy looked up at her father with frightened eyes. "Not even for Joey?"

There was a sudden strangling sound in Joe's throat. His eyes glistened with unbidden tears. "Joey will be just fine! Now go get dressed," he said hoarsely. He picked up a stick of wood and opened the top of the stove, keeping his back to his daugh-ters.

Mischief followed Hildy to where she stopped at the door to the dining room. "Daddy, somehow, I'll help you pay—"

"Joey is not your responsibility, Hildy. He's mine. Leave well enough alone."

Startled and hurt at her father's rough tone, Hildy hurried into the bedroom with her sister.

"He didn't mean anything by that," Elizabeth said, putting her arm around Hildy. "If we could put ourselves in his shoes, we'd see what he's going through."

Hildy fought back a warm rush of tears. She slipped her arms around Elizabeth and whispered, "I thought I was the big sister in this family."

"You are, but Molly says I'm the practical one."

"You're only ten years old," Hildy said softly, holding her sister tight. "Ten years going on thirty."

A little while later, Hildy pulled on her warm winter jacket. She headed down the long lane toward the country road and the school bus stop. She glanced toward the distant ranch house. Hildy's thoughts jumped from concern about her brother to the mysterious girl she'd seen.

I wonder if Brother Ben is right? Is that outlaw gang hiding out there? Is that girl I saw really Huxley Stonecipher's daughter?

Hildy shook her head, unable to comprehend how a man could be spiteful enough to kidnap his own daughter, especially just to get even with his ex-wife.

Wonder what the girl's name is? Hildy mused, still looking toward the two-story house. *Boy, I sure would like to talk to her! But how?*

In spite of her jacket, Hildy shivered in the crisp morning air. The weak sun peeked through the clouds and reflected off the shiny top of her lunch pail. The pail had originally held a pound of lard. Now it contained her lunch—a bologna sandwich, a boiled egg, and a small orange. It was a lot better than what she sometimes had to eat.

Hildy was lost in thought about Joey, the mysterious girl, and what Brother Ben had said about the outlaws, so she wasn't aware of a car approaching until it was almost even with her. She glanced up, startled.

Matthew Farnham was nattily dressed in his dark banker's suit. He smiled at Hildy from the window of his Pierce Arrow. A fourteen-year-old freckle-faced boy sat beside the banker. The boy wore an aviator's cap like the one Charles Lindbergh wore seven years before, when he flew the Atlantic alone in a single-engine airplane.

"Spud!" Hildy cried in delight.

"Get in," the banker called, sticking his head out the window. "We'll give you a lift to school."

"Yeah!" Spud added, "We have big news for you!"

Oh-oh! Hildy thought, suddenly feeling scared. *I hope they haven't found out that Brother Ben is right—that the outlaw gang does live next to us!*

Chapter Four

A DARING PLAN

Tuesday

Hildy leaned over and stuck her head inside the open window on the passenger's side. "What big news?" she asked, looking into Spud's green eyes.

"Get in and we'll tell you," he said, scooting over toward the driver to make room. "You won't have to ride the bus today. We'll take you directly to your school."

Hildy had looked forward to seeing Ruby on the bus and talking about last night, but Spud's big grin and invitation were too much to resist. She opened the door and slid onto the leather seat. She placed her lunch pail on the floor and looked expectantly at Spud.

His face and the backs of his hands were covered with freckles. Reddish hair curled out from under his aviator's cap. His voice raised with excitement, almost cracking, as he triumphantly announced, "My old man signed the papers!"

"The guardianship papers?" Hildy asked. When Spud nodded, she cried, "Oh, Spud, I'm so happy for you!"

"Thanks. Now it's official," he said. "Mr. Farnham's my legal guardian."

The banker said, "Remember, Spud, we agreed something less formal than *mister* is appropriate now." He was a small, dapper man, with a heavy gold watch chain stretched across his vest. He eased the big car back onto the graveled road, heading toward town.

"Right, Uncle Matt!" Spud replied. He looked at Hildy and smiled. "He's my honorary uncle."

"That's wonderful," Hildy said, showing her sense of relief and happiness. "Now you won't ever have to go hoboing again!"

"No," he said, a tinge of bitterness in his voice. "And I won't ever have to worry about my old man getting drunk and beating up on me either!"

Hildy turned away from the pain in the boy's eyes and the memory of the one thing she'd done to help that had backfired.

Two years ago Spud had run away from home with no companion except his dog Lindy, and joined the thousands of jobless men "riding the rods" of freight trains and living in hobo "jungles." After Hildy and Spud became friends, she had persuaded him to return to his home and try to patch things up.

Soon Spud was back in California, saying his father hadn't changed and never would. When his father got drunk and started beating him, Spud left again. He returned to see Hildy, saying she and her family were the only real friends he ever had. Then he met Matthew Farnham, his wife, and children. They all took a liking to the boy and Mr. Farnham applied to be Spud's legal guardian.

Hildy sighed, looking through the window at the slowly changing barren countryside. Ranch houses with trees now dotted the land. Rolling brown hills were replaced by irrigated green alfalfa fields and acres of ladino clover.

"Oh!" Hildy exclaimed, breaking away from the view to face the two again. "Mr. Farnham, I was so excited about the guardianship papers that I forgot to tell you something."

She quickly recounted the story of the new girl and the armed men at the old abandoned ranch house, and the threat the man had made to Hildy through the door.

Mr. Farnham said, "Ben called me last night after your uncle and cousin had been to your house, Hildy. Ben told me about the possibility that the bank robber Hux Stonecipher and his gang might be using that old house as their hideout."

"And planning to rob your gold train," Hildy said.

"It's not my gold train," the banker replied. "It's an independently owned short line. But gold from my mine—along with other mines around Quartz City—is shipped on that narrow-gauge railroad about twenty miles to Colfax. There it's transferred to the regular standard-gauge railroad for the final leg of the journey to the mint in San Francisco."

Spud explained, "Last night Ben told Uncle Matt that his law-enforcement contacts at Quartz City have found a stool pigeon."

"What does that mean?" Hildy asked.

"It's an informant—someone who tells the police something he knows that they don't. The police caught this *stoolie* after an armed robbery of a store in Quartz City. He was on parole and knew he'd get extra prison time."

Spud was mostly self-educated and loved to use big words. He continued, "So this informant tried to make a deal with the police, claiming he was a former member of Stonecipher's gang, but had an altercation with the leader."

"Now the informant wants to get even," Hildy guessed, "by turning the gang in. Or getting the leader caught, anyway. Plus getting a lighter sentence for helping the police."

Spud nodded. "The only problem is that the stoolie left the gang before they decided when and where to rob that train."

"So they're going to try it?" Hildy asked.

The banker shook his head. "Maybe, maybe not. The informant may have been lying."

Matt Farnham slowed the Pierce Arrow as they reached the city limits. Hildy leaned forward in the seat. "Do you suppose that's really Stonecipher's gang living near us?"

The banker shook his head. "I doubt it. Mine's the only bank around here, and it's too small to be worth the bother of a big-time robber like Stonecipher. Ben and I are agreed that if Stonecipher is hiding out here, he's after a more lucrative target."

"Like the gold train?" Hildy guessed.

Mr. Farnham nodded. "It all ties together. The hard-rock or quartz mines are only about a three-hour drive from here. But I really can't bring myself to believe that any gang would try robbing that train."

"Oh?" Hildy said. "Why not?"

"Mostly because it's impractical. That's why nobody's ever tried to rob it in the sixty-five years it's been hauling millions of dollars worth of gold. For instance, bullion is shipped in ingots weighing eighty-nine pounds apiece. It's too hard to cart away a whole carload of ingots weighing that much.

"Besides," the banker continued, "those shipments are heavily guarded. Banks aren't so well protected. They're being robbed all over the country."

Spud said, "Since the G-men got John Dillinger last summer, I hear that Hux Stonecipher's about the worst outlaw left alive."

"Two more things," Mr. Farnham added. "Even if a gang succeeded in stopping the train and somehow overpowering the guards, it would take several trucks to haul the gold away. Then they'd have the problem of disposing of it. By law, in this country, gold can be sold only to our government for thirty-five dollars a troy ounce. That's not what crooks would do. They know it's worth seven hundred dollars an ounce on the world market. It could be smuggled to Mexico, but that's about a thousand miles from the gold country.

"So even if the outlaws did get their hands on the gold, they'd never be able to drive their loaded trucks that distance. Police would be watching every road. No, I just don't see how any gang would be so foolish as to think they could rob the train and get away with the gold."

Hildy asked, "But would that keep them from trying?"

"I think so," Mr. Farnham answered. "Unless they've thought of a different way to get the gold to Mexico. Anyway, I told Ben to keep his eyes open. If there is going to be a robbery attempt, whether on my bank or the gold train, I'd like to be able to stop it and put the crooks in jail."

"Brother Ben might know more about them today," Hildy

said. Her thoughts jumped. "I wonder why Brother Ben came by yesterday? He never did say, just that it would keep. And I wonder what Dad will do about Joey—" Hildy broke off sharply, realizing she'd made a slip of the tongue. So far, she hadn't said anything about Joey's fever and his suddenly becoming unconscious.

"What about Joey?" the banker asked, turning into the side street that led to the Northside School for seventh and eighth graders.

Thinking fast, Hildy remembered that her father had only said that he would not borrow money from the banker for surgery, if that's what Joey needed.

"Well," Hildy began, recounting the scare Joey had given the family yesterday.

When she finished, the banker eased the Pierce Arrow up to the curb by the school. "Hildy, tell your father to come see me."

She picked up her lunch pail and opened the car door. "He won't do that."

"Why not?" Mr. Farnham asked.

Hildy stepped from the running board to the sidewalk, then turned and bent to look through the open window. "I'm sorry, but I can't say."

As the car pulled away, Hildy waved, then turned from the two-story red-brick school building to wait by the bus sheds. She and Ruby usually rode the bus together, so Hildy knew where to wait for it. When the bus pulled up, Hildy met Ruby as she stepped off, her lunch pail catching the sunlight.

"How'd ye git here a-fore me?" Ruby asked.

"Mr. Farnham and Spud gave me a lift," Hildy replied, motioning for Ruby to walk away from the rest of the students. "They told me what happened last night after you left my place and saw Brother Ben."

Hildy briefly recounted the rest of the conversation with Spud and Mr. Farnham.

Ruby shook her short, blonde hair. "Ain't it jist too bad we cain't find out fer shore 'bout that thar man who wouldn't open the door fer ye yesti'dy? I mean, whether or not he is that Stonecipher feller, an' also whether those men with guns were hunters or crooks."

"I thought about that while waiting for your bus," Hildy replied. "There may be a way," she said slowly. "If I could just talk to that girl I saw, maybe I could learn something, one way or another."

"Ain't no way ye kin do that."

"Yes, there is."

"They is?" Ruby questioned. "How?"

"We could go over there tonight after school and watch for her. If she rides her bike around behind the barn, nobody from the house could see us, and—"

"Hold it! Ye ain't gonna talk me into no such tomfool notion as that!"

"Why not? If we're careful, nobody'll see us."

"But what if'n they do? You said them men had guns. No, sireee! I ain't a-gonna do it."

Hildy was disappointed and asked, "You mean because you're scared?"

A flush spread across Ruby's cheeks. She glared at Hildy and answered, "I ain't skeered o' nothin' I kin see! Jist haints and sich like. They skeer me."

"I've told you a thousand times—there are no such things as haunts or ghosts or anything like that. Those were just men I saw, and they can't hurt us if they don't see us. Now, will you come with me tonight?"

Ruby groaned. "I reckon I'm a-gonna be sorry—but jist this once!"

"Great!" Hildy exclaimed, hurrying toward the school building. "We'll get to the bottom of this mystery together!"

Ruby ran alongside, shaking her head. "I jist hope we'uns don't end up bein' *part* of that ol' mystery!"

Hildy remembered the man's warning through the crack in the front door—to stay away. She swallowed hard. Under her breath, she muttered, "Me too."

Chapter Five

BAD NEWS

Tuesday Afternoon and Night

That afternoon, when Hildy opened the front door to the house, she immediately smelled fish. Then she remembered the apricot tree that had seemed to blossom with salmon.

Mischief waddled toward her mistress, chirring with pleasure. Hildy picked up the raccoon and called out. Nobody answered, although she could hear Sarah and Iola playing in the backyard. Hildy put her lunch pail and books on the dining room table on her way to the kitchen.

"Whew, Dad!" she exclaimed, fanning her right hand in front of her face. "That smells awful!"

Her father looked up from the wood-burning stove. He used a pair of long-handled tongs to lift a sealed glass jar from the metal boiler, the same one Molly used to add bluing to the family wash.

"It's from cleaning the salmon," he explained through the steam rising from the boiler. He carefully lowered the jar into an old lug box sitting on the bench that usually served for seating at the table. "These canned fish will taste great this winter."

Hildy had her doubts, so she decided to change the subject. "Where's Molly and Joey?"

"Ben took them to see Mrs. Radcliffe. They're not back yet." Hildy's father straightened up and gingerly reached for another jar with the tongs. He had learned how to cook and can during the years of moving from place to place seeking work. He added, "Good thing Ben came by, because I've been canning all day and I'm still not done."

Hildy lifted Mischief from her favorite perch astride her neck and carefully loosened the coon's nimble forepaws from her braids. "I'll get changed and help you," she said.

"I'd be obliged if you'd carry those fish heads and innards out behind the barn."

"Oh, Dad!" Hildy protested, wrinkling her nose. "I'll smell like fish for a week!"

"I've already put them in a bucket. You won't have to touch anything but the handle. I've dug a hole, too, and left the shovel there so you can cover everything."

Hildy still didn't like the chore, but after she changed from her school clothes, she carried the smelly pail outside. Her two younger sisters wanted to tag along, but Hildy said no. However, Mischief followed at a rolling run, protesting the fact that she wasn't given any of the pail's contents. Hildy rounded the barn and stopped in surprise.

A red-haired girl wearing a royal blue beret stood with her back to Hildy, peering into the hole Joe Corrigan had dug. Suddenly, the girl whirled in alarm.

"Hi!" Hildy greeted her with a smile. "You must be the new girl who moved into that house across the field. My cousin Ruby and I were going over to—. Wait! Where are you going?"

The stranger lifted her long, floral-print dress above her knees and dashed across the open pasture.

"Wait!" Hildy called. "Come back! I want to talk to you."

The red-haired girl continued on with the speed of a frightened jackrabbit. Hildy watched as she reached the edge of a dry irrigation ditch. She plunged in and was out of sight.

Gaining her wits about her, Hildy set down her pail and ran to the ditch bank where the girl had disappeared. She stopped, gasping for breath. The dirt bottom was cracked and dried, leaving no tracks. A few broken cattails showed where the girl had run by.

Hildy lifted her eyes, following the canal to where it ended and the acres of wheat stubble began. She glimpsed the girl sprinting toward the fence that separated the irrigated pasture land from the wheat stubble. She could see the neighbor's sagging barn beyond that.

Hildy turned back toward Mischief, thinking, *Whoever that girl is, she certainly didn't want to talk to me. I wonder if she really is that outlaw's daughter?*

Hildy retraced her steps to the hole behind the barn. Mischief had succeeded in dumping most of the contents of the galvanized pail and was standing in the mess.

Hildy groaned. "Oh, no! Look at you! You won't be able to come into the house until you have a bath."

Hildy jumped back as the coon turned and tried to place her forepaws on Hildy's legs. This was the little animal's way of begging to be picked up. "Don't touch me! And you can't ride on my neck, either. You'll walk to the house and wait outside."

Hildy quickly dumped the rest of the fish entrails into the hole and headed for the house. Mischief followed several paces behind, complaining loudly. Hildy stopped at the tank house to rinse out some of the offensive fish odor from the bucket. She had just turned on the faucet when Sarah and Iola ran up shouting that Brother Ben was driving up the lane with Molly and Joey.

Hildy gave Mischief a quick rubdown with an old gunnysack and grabbed her little sisters' hands. "Come on! Let's go hear what Mrs. Radcliffe said about Joey."

With Sarah and Iola in tow, Hildy ran around the shack. In her anxiety to know about Joey, Hildy forgot about the strange girl who had run away.

When the Packard stopped, Hildy stepped onto the running

board and stuck her head through the open window. As soon as she saw Molly's face she knew.

Bad news! Hildy told herself with a sudden feeling of dread. *I can see it in Molly's eyes.*

Hildy's father came hurrying from the house, wiping his rough hands on an old towel. His face was impassive as he opened the door, took his son in his arms, and helped Molly out of the car.

Nobody spoke until Joey pulled on his right ear and said, "Hurt."

Hildy held out her arms to him, but he twisted away, reaching for his stepmother. She took him back from her husband as the old ranger came around from the driver's side and stood with the family.

Molly said softly, "Joe, I think Sarah and Iola should go play by themselves now."

Joe nodded and sent the two protesting little sisters around to the back of the house. Hildy and the others went inside.

Molly began, "Mrs. Radcliffe said she's seen many similar cases—earache, fussiness, fever, sometimes passing out from a seizure, like Joey did."

"What does she think it is?" Hildy asked fearfully.

Molly replied, "She says it can happen almost any time from a child's first winter until they're about four. There's a canal from the middle ear called the eustachian tube. Liquid from there sometimes gets into the middle ear, which is an air-filled space. The fluid causes pressure against the eardrum; infection sets in, causing pain and fever."

Ben added, "Mrs. Radcliffe said that home remedies include applying hot compresses, blowing smoke in the ear, or dropping warm mineral oil in it. But none of these really helps."

"What does help?" Hildy's father asked.

"A doctor can lance the area to drain the infection," Molly answered.

Her husband asked, "You mean, an operation?"

Molly nodded soberly. "If the infection goes on too long, the eardrum can burst and allow the infection into the mastoids, which are bone cells in the skull. If the infection eats through to the brain—" Molly's voice trailed off.

Hildy didn't want to hear the rest.

But her father asked cautiously, "Are you saying that if the infection gets into Joey's brain, he'll die?"

Molly nodded, hugging Joey tight. "Maybe Mrs. Radcliffe is wrong. Only a doctor can tell for sure." She blinked away tears.

Hildy stared at her little brother in numbed disbelief.

The old ranger cleared his throat. "I told Molly that I'd be glad to help—"

Hildy's father interrupted bruskly. "I'm obliged, Ben, but Joey's my responsibility."

"I understand," Ben replied. "If you'll excuse me, I'll be on my way."

After Ben left, the Corrigan household took on an unnatural quietness. Hildy went out back and helped her two sisters finish cleaning and drying Mischief, praying silently as she did. Even when Elizabeth and Martha came home from school, they seemed to quickly understand that something was seriously wrong with Joey, though no one mentioned any details.

Hildy was so preoccupied that she didn't think about the fact that Ruby should have already been there. It would be dark by five o'clock, and too late to carry out Hildy's plan for her and Ruby to find the mystery girl outside of the old house.

After supper, when Ruby arrived with her father, Hildy led her cousin aside and whispered, "It's already dark! We can't go see that girl now."

Ruby explained, "Muh daddy was a-workin' on his sermon, and he wouldn't quit, no matter how hard I pestered him to drive me over here."

"Well, she was here."

"She was? When? Whar?"

"This afternoon, out behind our barn." In a low voice, Hildy quickly explained how she had found the girl looking into the hole her father had dug, but that she'd run away when she spoke to her.

Ruby frowned. "I'd shore admire to talk to her, but it's too dark fer us to be a-goin' over now."

Hildy said, "We'll have to try another time, maybe tomorrow. Oh, I just remembered! I forgot to cover the hole behind the barn. I'd better do it now, or Mischief will get into that fish again."

"I'll he'p ye," Ruby said. "Ye got an extry shovel?"

"There's one with a broken handle in the barn. I'll use that, and you can use the other."

The cousins put on warm coats, lit the lantern, and stepped out into the cool night. The pale yellow light swinging past their legs made huge shadows on the side of the barn as they approached. Hildy told Ruby what Mrs. Radcliffe had said about Joey's ear infection.

Just before she finished they reached the barn, and Hildy slid the heavy door open enough to step inside. The sagging structure smelled of hay and dust. Pigeons stirred on their rafter perches beneath the center of the peaked roof. Hildy raised the lantern high to better locate the shovel. She saw it leaning against the end of a broken wooden manger.

Ruby asked, "Whatcha gonna do 'bout Joey?"

"I'm praying he doesn't have any more of those seizures or spells, and that he'll be all right."

"What if he ain't?"

Hildy picked up the broken shovel. "Joey will need an operation."

"I know yore daddy. He never cottoned much to doctors. An' more so since he blamed them for lettin' yore ma die. I reckon bein' laid off, an' havin' no cash money lays a perty heavy load on him."

"Brother Ben offered to help—to pay the doctor," Hildy said, carrying the lantern and shovel across the barn floor. "But Daddy refused. And the banker could lend us the money, but Daddy wouldn't take it, I know that."

Ruby observed, "Yore daddy's a mighty proud man—wants to take keer o' his own. Cain't blame him fer that."

"There must be something I can do to help," Hildy said sadly. "There's got to be—. Listen!" Hildy stopped abruptly, cocking her head and holding her breath.

Ruby stood stock still beside her. After a long silence, she whispered, "I don't hear nothin.' "

"I did! It's outside!"

"Ye reckon Mischief follered us?"

"No," Hildy whispered back. "I heard footsteps."

"Footsteps? Ain't nobody else out here!"

"Maybe that red-haired girl came back. Come on, let's find out."

Hildy set the lantern on the barn floor. "We'd better leave the light here," she whispered. "I don't want to scare her again."

Ruby muffled a frightened sound. "What if'n it's a haint instead of that thar gal?"

"How many times do I have to tell you there's no such thing as a haunt? Give me your hand."

Ruby reluctantly placed her hand in Hildy's, protesting between clenched teeth, "How do ye figger on slippin' up on somebody in the dark?"

"Shh!" Hildy hissed. "Come on. I think the footsteps were on this side of the barn."

Outside, with only pale shafts of lantern light showing through the cracks, Hildy had second thoughts. She couldn't see anything except the black sky, with a few flickering cold, distant stars. A brisk wind was up, and it cut through her jacket like a keen-edged knife.

Is it the cold or fear that's giving me goosebumps? Hildy asked herself as she held Ruby's hand.

Ruby leaned close and whispered, "I jist thought o' somethin'. Supposin' it ain't that thar gal a-tall, but one o' them outlaws? Maybe even the leader—what's his name? Hux Stone—something?"

"Shh!" Hildy commanded hoarsely.

Ruby made a low, moaning sound. "Lookee yonder! I see somethin' a-movin'! Either it's that thar crook or a haint! We better turn tail and skedaddle fer the house!"

"Wait!" Hildy clung tightly to her cousin, holding her back. Hildy swallowed hard as she heard a voice in the darkness.

Chapter Six

A DANGEROUS REQUEST

Tuesday Night

It was a girl's voice: "Hi!"

Hildy let out her breath in a relieved rush and exclaimed to Ruby, "It's that girl!"

It was hard to make out her features in the darkness, but Hildy raised her voice: "Hi, I'm Hildy Corrigan. This is my cousin, Ruby Konning."

"I'm Dixie Mae—uh, just Dixie Mae." She stepped closer to the girls.

"Let's go inside the barn where it's light," Hildy suggested.

"I can't stay long," Dixie Mae replied, following Hildy and Ruby toward the shafts of light the lantern cast through cracks in the barn.

Inside, Hildy picked up the lantern and hung it on a nail in the wall. She turned to look at the girl again, who was about Hildy's height and age. She wore the same long, flower-print dress, covered now by a man's bulky waist-length coat. She had sad, hazel eyes, and lots of freckles like Spud. Her hair was a golden red, whereas Spud's was a darker shade.

"I shouldn't have run away this afternoon, but I was scared he'd see me," Dixie Mae began nervously, looking imploringly at Hildy. "So I had to come back."

"Who's *he*?" Hildy asked.

Dixie Mae chewed at her fingernails, then answered, "My father. We just moved into that old place next door. He doesn't like me talking to strangers."

"How come?" Ruby asked.

The girl didn't seem to hear. She paced like a cat, eyes darting furtively through the open barn windows that faced the distant county road. "Fact is, he won't even let me go to school, and if he knew I was here, he'd skin me alive! I've got to get back before he returns."

She smiled wanly at Hildy. "You seemed friendly this afternoon, so I—well, I slipped over here and waited, hoping I'd see you. I just have to talk to somebody!" The words gushed out as though she were bursting with thoughts that needed to be released. She added, "I didn't scare you two just now, did I?"

"Naw!" Ruby scoffed. "We wasn't skeered!"

Hildy gave her cousin an amused look, then said to the new girl, "I'd seen you a couple of times, so I went to your house, but—"

"I know," Dixie Mae interrupted. "I'm sorry Daddy ran you off." She stopped pacing and glanced cautiously around. "Can I ask you both something?"

Hildy and Ruby exchanged glances while the red-haired girl stepped into the shadows. She started biting her fingernails again.

Hildy noticed the girl's nails were extremely short. "Go ahead," Hildy urged. "What did you want to ask?"

Dixie Mae searched the girls' faces as though she were trying to decide if they could be trusted. "Will you both cross your hearts and hope to die that you won't tell anybody else?"

Hildy answered carefully, "We can't promise without knowing what it is."

The girl looked suddenly stricken. "I was afraid you'd say that," she said sadly. "I shouldn't have come." She turned toward the barn door.

"Hey, wait!" Hildy cried, reaching out to touch the girl's shoulder. "Maybe we can help if you'll trust us."

"Yeah!" Ruby agreed. "An' if'n we cain't, ye might feel a whole sight better jist fer sayin' it."

Dixie Mae considered Ruby's words with a frown. "Maybe you're right." She walked over to the broken-down manger and gingerly sat on the edge of it. "I thought about this a lot since this afternoon, but I don't know how to begin."

"Jist spit it out," Ruby urged. "I reckon that's 'bout the best way thar is to git started."

Dixie Mae thought a moment, then nodded slowly. "Okay, here goes. My mother and father were divorced some years back, and Mom got custody of me 'cause he's, uh—my daddy's been away a lot. I hadn't seen him in years, but—you're not going to believe this part, but it's true—Daddy kidnapped me a few days ago when I was walking home from school."

Dixie Mae pushed herself up from the manger and looked imploringly at Hildy and Ruby. "He brought me out here, clear across the country! But he doesn't treat me right. He—" She couldn't go on, or thought better of it.

Hildy asked softly, "He hits you, doesn't he?"

The girl gingerly touched her upper left arm with her right hand, as though feeling a bruise, even through her thick coat. "How'd you know?"

"It doesn't matter," Hildy answered. "What do you want me and Ruby to do?"

"I just want to get home to Mom in New York." Dixie Mae began pacing again. "But there's no way I can get away from Daddy by myself—can you help?"

Ruby was adamant. "Ye realize what yo're a-askin' us to do? Why, if'n we he'p, yore daddy could come after Hildy an' me! An' if he hauls off and whangs his own flesh an' blood, what do ye reckon he'd do to us?"

"I promise you won't get into any trouble," Dixie Mae said earnestly. "Not if you'll help me with the plan I've worked out."

"What's that?" Hildy asked.

"Well," the girl said, hope beginning to show in her eyes, "Daddy and some men who—uh—work with him, come and go a lot. While they're gone, I can slip over here. If you can find some way to get me into the county seat where the motor stage stops, and can loan me the money for a ticket, my mom will pay you back when I get home. Honest, she will! Please, will you help me?"

Ruby muttered, "We'uns ain't got no cash money! Fact o' the matter is, in these hard times, our daddies ain't got none neither."

"Hold on, Ruby," Hildy cut in. "Dixie Mae, even if we helped you get home, what's to keep your father from kidnapping you again?"

The girl's shoulders sagged like a suddenly emptied gunnysack. She sank down on the edge of the manger again, bowing her head almost to her knees. "Oh," she whispered, her voice filled with anguish. "I hadn't thought of that."

Hildy walked over and knelt in front of her. "Do you love your father?" she asked.

Dixie Mae raised her head and brushed the hair from her face. The lantern light made her tears glisten as she answered, "I think so. Because he's my father. But he doesn't love me. He told me he took me from Mom just to spite her because she divorced him. I've got to get away from him and back to Mom. I'm desperate! Won't you please help me?"

"You're Huxley Stonecipher's daughter, then?" Hildy asked evenly.

The girl flinched. She started to shake her head, then said, "How did you guess?"

Hildy didn't want to bring Brother Ben into it, so she just shrugged. "Let's just say we know about your father's—uh—work."

Dixie Mae's eyes widened in surprise. "Does that mean you'll help me?"

Hildy nodded, having no idea how it could be arranged, but feeling great compassion for the girl. "We'll help you, but we can't do it alone. We'll need some grown-ups to—"

"No, no!" Dixie Mae's voice shot up. "They'll go to the police, and they're liable to hurt my daddy! I couldn't live with myself if that happened. I just want to get back to my mother."

"Listen," Hildy began, looking into Dixie Mae's eyes. "There is no way Ruby and I can help you alone. But believe me, you can trust the grown-ups that we'll ask to help."

Dixie Mae nibbled on a fingernail. "You're sure?" When both Hildy and Ruby nodded, she added, "Promise?"

"We promise," the cousins replied together.

Dixie Mae looked nervous again. "I have to go now," she said, moving quickly toward the barn door. "They'll be back soon, and I have to be inside before they are."

Hildy grabbed the girl's coat sleeve. "We'll need to talk again—you know, to make arrangements. Can you come back here tomorrow night about the same time?"

"I don't know. I'll try. If I don't make it, you could slip over to our barn. I can go that far, even when they're home. I've got to go now!"

Hildy lifted the lantern from the nail. "Don't worry. Everything will turn out all right."

Dixie Mae stepped outside. "Do you really believe that, or are you just trying to make me feel better?"

Hildy looked up, past the pinpoint stars that were sprinkled overhead in the dark sky. "I learned a verse in Sunday school once: 'All things are possible to him who believes.' I'm going to believe that you'll soon be safely back home with your mother."

Dixie Mae repeated part of the verse softly, "All things are possible—I like that. I hope it's true. Thanks, both of you, for helping me." She turned quickly and disappeared around the barn.

Hildy and Ruby did not speak as they hurried back to the tar-paper shack. Inside the kitchen, they found the four little sisters washing up before bed.

Elizabeth spoke up. "You two sure took an awfully long time to bury those smelly fish heads."

Hildy gasped and covered her mouth.

Ruby blurted, "We clean fergot!"

"You forgot what you went out to do?" the incredulous ten-year-old asked in surprise. "What've you been doing then?"

"Never mind," Hildy answered, taking off her coat. "I'll go out later. Come on, Ruby. We've got to talk to our fathers."

"About what?" Elizabeth asked, following the cousins into the dining room.

"It ain't none o' yore beeswax," Ruby replied.

"I'll bet you're in some kind of trouble," Elizabeth persisted. "You two are always getting into trouble."

Hildy turned to whisper in her little sister's ear. "I'll tell you later, but the other girls are too young to know. Now, how about taking them back into the kitchen to finish washing up?"

"Well," Elizabeth said, obviously feeling important for having been trusted with even that bit of information. "I guess I can wait." She herded the younger girls, who had followed, back into the kitchen and closed the door behind them.

Nate and Joe looked up as Hildy and Ruby entered the living room. Hildy had noticed that Molly was sitting on the edge of her bed, watching Joey asleep in his lug-box crib. Hildy knew Molly would be able to hear what she was going to say.

"Dad, Uncle Nate," Hildy began. "Ruby and I have something to tell you." The two quickly related their meeting with Dixie Mae, and then answered a few questions.

Hildy's father took a slow, deep breath, letting it out fast. "Now that we know for sure that outlaw is living next door, we'd better tell Ben Strong. He'll know better than any of us the best way to deal with this. I'll get my hat."

"No, Joe," Nate replied quickly. "You stay here with your family—just in case—I mean, your place is here. Ruby and I have to be going anyway. We'll drive over to Brother Ben's right now."

"I'm obliged," Joe Corrigan said. "Would you mind asking

him to come out here tonight and tell us what he thinks we should do? I'll wait up."

When Hildy's uncle and cousin had driven off in their borrowed Model T Ford, Hildy went to check on her baby brother.

He slept on a pile of old clothes that served as a mattress in the little lug-box crib. Molly still sat on the edge of her bed, looking down helplessly at the child. Hildy could see the concern on her stepmother's face even by the faint light offered by the living room lamp.

"How is he?" Hildy asked softly.

"Restless." Molly sighed and stood up. "He keeps pulling at his ear and tossing and turning."

For a long moment, Hildy stood in thoughtful silence, her eyes tenderly beholding her only brother. *We've got to find a way to help Joey have that operation!* she told herself with firm resolve.

Molly motioned for Hildy to follow her out into the living room. Joe Corrigan sat in the old rocker, elbows on his knees and head in his hands. He looked up at his wife and daughter.

Molly seemed to read the question in his eyes, for she volunteered the information that Joey was sleeping but restless, then added, "I overheard what all of you were saying about the girl next door. I hate to think what that terrible man might do to us if he knows we tried to help his daughter get away from him."

Hildy's father stood and took his wife's hand. "If she were our girl, wouldn't you want somebody to help her?"

"Of course I would," Molly said, sliding into the circle of Joe's arms. "But the man is a killer! He belongs back in jail. Why on earth is he living next to us?"

Hildy's father said matter-of-factly, "He's hiding out from the law."

"But why here?" Molly asked again.

Her husband shrugged, and Hildy rolled the thought around in her mind: *Why didn't I think to ask Dixie Mae that?*

Molly's voice was weak and trembling. "If something goes wrong, and that man comes after us, we've got nobody to help us way out here in the country. We don't even have a telephone!"

Hildy put her arms around her father and stepmother. "It's going to be all right, I just know it."

Molly shook her head. "Nothing is going to be all right until that man and his gang are behind bars!"

Hildy considered that along with Dixie Mae's statement that she didn't want her father hurt, even though he had hit her and had inflicted emotional pain on his ex-wife by kidnapping Dixie Mae.

Hildy went to the back door, slipped her coat on, and went out to the barn again to finally bury the fish entrails. When she returned to the living room, she sat quietly with her father and stepmother to wait for Brother Ben.

Hildy peered out the window at the old house and shivered, but not from cold.

Chapter Seven

SOUNDS IN THE NIGHT

Tuesday Night and Wednesday

Hildy had thought she was too excited and concerned to sleep, but she awoke on the living room couch with a start. Before falling asleep she'd undone her braids, and now her hair covered her eyes. She jumped up, smoothed her dress, and brushed her hair back from her face just as her father and stepmother opened the door for Ben Strong.

He tiptoed into the living room so that the sound of his cowboy boots wouldn't wake the sleeping children. His big white Stetson hat in his right hand, he said in his soft drawl, "Sorry to be so late, folks. After Nate and Ruby told me what this Dixie Mae girl had to say, I had some thinking to do. Didn't want to make a mistake. This case is too risky to make a single wrong move."

"What did you decide?" Hildy's father asked, sitting down in the old upholstered chair.

Molly took the rocker while the old ranger sat down on the couch. Placing his hat on the frayed arm of the couch, he patted the cushion beside him. Hildy sat down, bursting with eagerness to hear his answer.

"My first question was why is Hux Stonecipher here?"

"We've been wondering the same thing," Hildy said.

"There has to be more to it than just a place to hide out," Ben continued. "I think he's getting ready to do something big."

"Like what?" Molly asked.

"Well, his usual pattern is to rob a bank."

Hildy exclaimed, "Mr. Farnham owns the only bank around here!"

Ben nodded. "I called him and alerted him. But I suspect Stonecipher's after a bigger prize."

"Such as?" Hildy's father prompted.

The old ranger leaned back on the couch. "Do you all remember the rumors my law-enforcement contacts have picked up from a police informant in the gold country?"

"Do you really think Dixie Mae's father is planning to rob the gold train?" Hildy asked.

"It's a possibility," the old ranger replied.

Hildy's father looked doubtful. "If nobody's attempted to rob that train in the sixty years or more that it's been hauling gold, why would a bank robber try now?"

"Maybe because if they could pull it off, they'd have so much money they'd never have to work another day in their lives," Ben replied.

Intrigued as she was by that possibility, Hildy was more interested in helping Dixie Mae. She asked, "Did you tell the police who our new neighbors are?"

"No, I didn't, and for good reasons. First, Ruby told me that you girls promised Dixie Mae she could trust the adults you'd get to help. I have to honor that.

"Next, if I told the local law-enforcement agencies, they'd call in the G-men. Then all three agencies would likely combine to surround the place. That might lead to a shoot-out and the girl could get hurt."

Hildy spoke up, "I promised to help her get away."

"So Ruby says." The old ranger gave his white walrus moustache a flip with the back of his right forefinger. "I decided to keep this to myself until I see if a little plan I have will work. Joe, how about if you take your family away for a few days?"

"Away? Where to?" he asked in surprise.

"My place. I may have to return to the gold country to follow up on this investigation with the police informant. Your family would have my house all to yourselves. Even if I don't go, there's plenty of room for all of us there. Either way, the outlaws wouldn't know where you were and you'd all be safe."

"I can't go because of another promise I made," Hildy said. "Dixie Mae might come over here tomorrow night. I've got to be here then."

"We are going to help the girl," Ben assured Hildy. "But in the meantime, I'd feel better if your family were away from danger until this thing is settled." Ben turned to Hildy's father. "Joe, maybe you could leave Molly and your younger children at my place, and you and I could stay here tomorrow night to protect Hildy and Ruby. If Dixie Mae shows up, we can take her and the girls to safety."

"Ruby?" Hildy asked in surprise.

Ben nodded. "Nate told me that Ruby can stay here with you. He says he has to prepare for his Sunday sermon."

Molly said, "Oh, I'd almost forgotten! We can't be away then. We need to be in the congregation to show our support for Nate, especially during his first sermon as the new pastor."

"Our family's protection comes first," Hildy's father declared.

Ben said, "You can drive to church from my house."

"How about it, Daddy?" Hildy asked.

Joe Corrigan was silent a long moment before saying, "Tell me what else is on your mind, Ben."

"Well, if I'm right about Stonecipher trying to rob the gold train, I'd like to catch him in the act. All we need to know is when and where he plans to hit the train. Maybe we can learn that from his daughter if she shows up here tomorrow night."

Hildy said, "Maybe she doesn't know."

"She may not," the old ranger agreed. "But if she can give us any idea of what he's up to, we can go from there. Of course, that depends on Hildy and Ruby being here tomorrow night to talk to Dixie Mae."

Molly voiced her fear of risking the girls' lives, but Hildy's father said he saw the logic of Ben's plan. "I know it's risky, Molly, but so is doing nothing when we know an outlaw gang is our nearest neighbor. We'll never be safe as long as they're around. Going away for a few days won't help in the long run; those men must be caught and jailed, and Hildy's the best person to help get the information."

Molly accepted her husband's decision and changed the subject. "Joe, what if Joey needs to see a doctor while we're away from you?"

Ben replied, "Naturally you could use my phone. And Joe," he managed to get in again, "I'll see to it that there's no doctor bill."

"Like I said before, Ben, I'm much obliged, but Joey's my responsibility."

Hildy wanted to cry, *Oh, Daddy, let Brother Ben help! We can't let Joey die!* But since it was useless to argue with her father, she kept quiet.

Ben said calmly, "I understand, Joe. But I don't think you would let pride get in the way of Joey's safety."

Hildy saw the lines in her father's face soften. He looked at Joey, and then at the old ranger. "I don't think we're in any danger yet. We'll stay here tonight, and move tomorrow when the girls get home from school."

"Good." Ben picked up his hat and stood. "I'd better be going. Oh, I almost forgot. Ruby said Dixie Mae also needed to borrow some money to get home to her mother. I'll see that she gets the amount when the time comes."

Molly said, "That's very kind of you, Brother Ben."

He shrugged, then turned to Hildy. "In case Dixie Mae shows up at your barn tomorrow night but won't come with us, we'll need a backup plan. First of all, you'll need to set another time to meet her so we can get her away from here. You better warn her that she must escape from the gang before there's a police raid on the place. Also, try to find out when and where her father is planning his next robbery. If it *is* the gold train, ask her if she knows the date and time they plan to attack, and how many men are in the gang. Tell her that I'll drive her directly to the airport in San Francisco."

"San Francisco?" Hildy was puzzled. "She only needs a ride to the motor stage stop in Dos Piedras."

The old ranger shook his head. "If something goes wrong and Stonecipher gets away, that's one of the first places he'd look. Dixie Mae will be home with her mother a lot faster flying on one of those new airliners that take off from the city. Once she's on her way, I'll send a telegram to her mother.

"Then I'll inform the law-enforcement people, and they'll move in on Stonecipher and his gang. Whether the authorities strike against the hideout next door, or try to nab them in a robbery attempt, there's almost sure to be a shootout. Before that happens, I want Dixie Mae safely away from here. Well, good-night, folks."

After the old ranger was gone, Hildy stood at the window, looking at the old house where the bandits lived. Her father and stepmother came up and stood beside her.

Hildy asked, "Daddy, if Dixie Mae comes with us tomorrow night, what do you think her father will do?"

"He'll look for her. Probably come here first, then check the stage depot, like Ben said. But from what Ruby told me, Stonecipher doesn't care enough about his own daughter to look very long. And the rest of the gang probably doesn't care a hoot about the girl. They just want the next robbery done so they can have the money. I doubt they'd let Stonecipher spend much time looking for the girl."

"I know he hits her," Hildy confided. "If he found her trying to get away, or caught Ruby and me—"

"He's not going to harm you," her father interrupted. "If all goes well, Dixie Mae will be back with her mother soon, and that gang will be behind bars. We've got a busy day tomorrow. Let's get some sleep."

Hildy spent a restless night, dreaming that she and Ruby had been caught by Dixie Mae's father as they tried to help the girl escape. The next morning Hildy was sleepy on the noisy bus ride to school. She wanted to talk with Ruby about the exciting events going on, but didn't dare say anything until they were alone.

It was noon before they could slip away for a private conversation. They found a bench against the backside of the bus sheds and pried the lids off their lunch buckets.

Suddenly, Hildy looked down the street. "That's Mr. Farnham's Pierce Arrow!" she exclaimed, jumping up so fast from the bench that she almost dumped her biscuit sandwich on the ground. "And Spud's with him."

Ruby mumbled something about Spud under her breath, but joined Hildy at the curb. As the car stopped, the girls bent to look in the window on the passenger's side. The dapper little banker at the wheel glanced around to be sure nobody was nearby. Then he leaned in front of Spud to speak to the girls.

"Ben and I met a while ago and reviewed what you talked about at your house last night, Hildy. We've had a slight change of plans. Do you girls have time to listen?"

"Sure!" Hildy replied for them both.

The banker explained, "Ben and I decided that if the girl agrees to leave tonight, she'll feel more comfortable if you and Ruby ride along to the airport."

"Good idee!" Ruby exclaimed. "I ain't never seen one o' them big airyplanes up close."

"I'll go along, too," Spud said. "Plenty of room for all of us. Once we're on the road, Ben can help the law capture Stonecipher and his gang, maybe even before they know Dixie Mae's gone. So what do you say?"

The cousins agreed to go if their parents would let them. The banker said he would ask them right away.

After Mr. Farnham and Spud left, Hildy and Ruby went back to their lunches and talked about all that had happened in the last few hours.

Ruby ended the conversation by saying, "I shore do hope nothin' goes wrong tonight. If'n Dixie Mae's daddy gits his hands on us—"

"He's not going to," Hildy assured her. But her voice was more firm than her convictions, and she was glad that her family would all leave the tar-paper shack that afternoon.

When Hildy and Ruby stepped off the bus at Hildy's stop, Ben Strong was waiting for them in his big Packard. The cousins jumped in and rode up the Corrigan's long driveway.

The moment Hildy opened the front door, she saw her father placing cardboard suitcases in the middle of the living room floor along with other family possessions. "Where's Joey?" she asked.

Her father greeted Ruby and Ben before answering Hildy. "Molly has Joey in the kitchen. He's all right."

"Thank God!" Hildy said fervently.

"We couldn't find your pet," Hildy's father said, "but she best stay here anyway. It would hardly be right to take a coon to Ben's place."

Ben said, "The raccoon is welcome, if you like."

"Thanks, Ben," Hildy said, "but Mischief will be all right here. She's probably out in the irrigation ditch now, looking for frogs or minnows in the little pools that are left."

Ben shrugged. "Suit yourself. Here, Joe, let me give you a hand with those things."

"Hildy and I can handle them," Joe said, then turning to his daughter, he spoke softly, "Hildy, I have some things to say to you."

As she and her father carried their meager possessions outside, he confided, "Hildy, I'm counting on you and Ruby to be mighty careful tonight. Ben and I will be inside, watching and listening. But if you sense you are in danger, use your head."

"I will," Hildy promised, feeling a slight chill at the hint that there may be a situation in which her father or the old ranger would not be able to help.

When everything was in the Packard, and Ben at the wheel, Hildy and her father said goodbye to Molly, the four little girls, and Joey. Hildy bent to kiss her brother, who was in Molly's arms.

"You be a good boy," Hildy said fondly, "and don't have any more fever. I'll see you soon."

As the yellow car eased down the dusty driveway, Hildy prayed silently. *Lord, take care of them all—especially Joey. And help Ruby and me when we meet with Dixie Mae tonight.*

After dark, when supper had been eaten and the dishes washed and put away, Ben returned to the shack to sit in silence and wait with Joe, Hildy, and Ruby. Hildy was glad but anxious when it was time to light the lantern and head toward the barn.

After she and Ruby had sat for a couple of hours against the manger in a vain effort to keep warm, Hildy stood and rubbed her gloved hands together. The cold had penetrated her clothes and she could feel it in her bones.

Ruby mused, "Somethin' musta happened, an' she ain't a-comin'."

"We'll give her another half hour or so," Hildy replied, stomping one foot and then the other.

"An' if she don't show?"

"Then we'll go on over to the barn on her place, like she suggested."

Ruby said hoarsely, "What if'n they made her tell 'bout the plan? Instead o' her a-comin' here, maybe one o' them bandits is a-sneakin' up on us right now!"

The thought alarmed Hildy, but she tried not to show it. "They won't. Listen!" She tensed, her eyes straining into the darkness beyond the slightly open barn door.

Chapter Eight

FEAR STALKS THE NIGHT

Wednesday Night

Hildy's heart thudded harder as she listened to the approaching sounds. She hadn't thought about an outlaw sneaking up on the barn until Ruby mentioned it. Now the possibility spurred Hildy to action. She glanced around for a weapon of some kind. When she looked again at the barn door, she saw two eyes glowing strangely in the pale lantern light.

Ruby croaked, "It's a haint!"

"No," Hildy replied with a big sigh of relief. She'd heard a familiar chirring sound. "It's Mischief!"

The raccoon entered the barn, waddling toward Hildy in the faint light.

Ruby let her breath out with a low, shuddering sound. "I knowed it was that ol' coon all the time," she announced with a slight quaver in her voice.

"Then why are your eyes as big as saucers?" Hildy teased, picking up her pet.

Ruby muttered, "Don't jist stand thar a-makin' fun o' me!

What air we gonna do 'bout meetin' Dixie Mae?"

Hildy put the animal down on the barn floor. "We're going over to her place, just like we said we would. Stay, Mischief! Come on, Ruby."

"Reckon we should tell yore daddy?"

Hildy shook her head. "There's no time. In fact, it might already be too late. But we have to try. Let's go!"

"What about the lantern?"

"Leave it. If we carry it across the open fields, somebody might see it."

The cousins slipped outside. They could see fairly well by the waning moonlight. Hildy led the way across the open pasture to the irrigation ditch. She and Ruby eased down into it, lowering the chances of someone from the outlaw's hideout seeing them.

The ditch ended at a barbed-wire fence that separated the irrigated pastures from the start of the rolling hills of wheat stubble. The girls bent low and carefully slipped between the strands of wire.

As Hildy straightened up, she heard something behind her. She froze, holding her breath and trying to hear above the sudden pounding of her heart. Her eyes probed the dark expanse of clover pasture.

Ruby whispered, "What is it?"

Hildy didn't answer for a moment, then replied, "I thought I heard something. It must have been my imagination." She looked toward the neighbor's barn. "There's a light inside," she whispered. "It's probably Dixie Mae waiting for us. But we'd better slip up quietly, just in case it's her father or some of his gang."

Hildy moved stealthily on tiptoe to the remnants of a corral. She followed the broken fence until she reached the barn. There she slipped quietly along the splintery wall to where a square of lantern light marked a window. Glancing quickly behind her to be sure Ruby was still with her, Hildy took another cautious step. Her foot struck a tin can, which bounced off the barn wall with a clatter. Hildy froze, not moving a muscle.

A girl's voice called softly from inside the barn: "Hildy, is that you?"

Hildy grabbed Ruby's hand. There was no pane in the window, so Hildy stuck her head in and grinned at Dixie Mae, who stood in the lantern light biting her nails. "Hi!" Hildy whispered.

"Climb in," Dixie Mae urged.

"No," Hildy answered. "We've come to take you away. You come out. We'll take you back to—"

"I can't!" Dixie Mae interrupted. "I've already been here a long time. My father will be calling for me any moment."

"We kin be long gone a-fore then!" Ruby whispered urgently. "If'n ye want to see yore mother, come now!"

Dixie Mae sobbed softly. "Oh, I want to do that, but I know my father! If he calls and I don't answer, he'll bring a light and come looking for me!"

Hildy was disappointed, but willing to face reality. "Well, we have to talk anyway. Come on, Ruby. Let's climb through the window."

Once inside, the three girls stood in shadows cast by the manger between them and the lantern on the wall. Hildy noticed Dixie Mae was wearing her royal blue beret again. She looked beyond the stanchions where cows had once been milked. The largest part of the barn was open and empty except for a layer of hay and a stack of old gunnysacks, while the far side of the building was too dark to see anything.

"There isn't much time," Hildy began, "so listen closely."

Hildy told Dixie Mae about Brother Ben's offer to provide the money for her trip home and the plans to drive them all to the airport in San Francisco. "Ruby and I will ride with you from our house. Let's go!"

"Oh, Hildy, Ruby. I told you—"

"Look!" Hildy interrupted, "You may not get another chance!" She turned toward the open barn window.

"Wait!" Dixie Mae protested. "I want to come, but I'm scared! Give me a second to think."

"Ain't no time fer thinkin'," Ruby muttered. "It's time to move—raht now!"

"Just one minute, please!" Dixie Mae pleaded.

Ruby grumbled, "If yo're so bound an' determined to stand thar a-wastin' time, why don't ye tell us why yore daddy an' his gang are here?"

"They don't talk around me. I didn't know what they were up to until this afternoon, when I overheard them talking about robbing a gold train."

Hildy glanced at Ruby, then back at Dixie Mae. "When? Where?"

"I don't know. All I heard was something about a tunnel in the foothills—"

She broke off as the screen door at the old house squeaked open. A man's gruff voice called, "Dixie Mae, time to come in!"

"That's my father," the girl whispered in a frightened tone.

Hildy motioned toward the open barn window. "Hurry! Come with us!"

"No!" Dixie Mae shook her head vigorously. "If I don't go in right away, he'll come looking for me. He'll catch you both, too!"

Hildy said, "We've got to ask you some questions, but we can do that on our way."

"Dixie Mae! You hear me?" The man's voice was louder and more fearsome. "Get in this house *now*!"

"Coming!" she called, then dropped her voice. "I'm sorry." She moved toward the lantern, speaking over her shoulder. "To-morrow night I'll come to your house as soon as I can. It may be late. Will you wait for me?"

Hildy was bitterly disappointed, but she felt compassion for the girl. "We'll wait," Hildy assured her.

"Dixie Mae!" The man's voice came in an angry roar. "You're asking for a hiding!"

"I'm coming!" she shouted. "Thanks," she whispered to Hildy and Ruby."

"It's okay," Hildy replied as the frightened girl left the barn quickly with the lantern. Then Hildy urged, "Ruby, crawl out the window. I'll be right behind you."

Hildy waited for her cousin to ease through the opening.

Ruby said softly, "I'm out. Boy, her father sounds meaner'n a rattlesnake with a sore tail."

"Shh!" Hildy cautioned in a hoarse voice. She reached up and started to climb through the window, then suddenly froze at the sound of movement in the straw behind her.

Ruby whispered, "I heerd somethin'. What ye reckon it is?"

Hildy didn't answer, straining to identify the sound. Her heart pounded and she had trouble breathing quietly.

"It's a-comin' this way!" Ruby croaked.

The familiar chirring sound reached Hildy's ears. She let out a big sigh of relief. "It's Mischief again! She followed us."

"Ye shore?" Ruby sounded doubtful.

"Yes." Hildy knelt down and reached out for the animal. "Come on, Mischief," she called softly.

The chirring sound came closer and Hildy felt the raccoon's soft fur in her hands. She lifted her pet gently and stood to the window. "Here," she said to Ruby. "I'll hand her over—oh-oh!"

Hildy froze as she heard the door at the far end of the barn slide open. A flashlight probed the opening, reflecting off three trucks and a long, cream-colored car. Hildy had seen a vehicle like that in Lone River recently. Her father had told her it was a new 1934 Cadillac sedan. Hildy guessed the one in the barn was a getaway car.

She crouched below the barn window, making herself as small as possible. She released Mischief as Ruby whispered from outside the open window. "Reckon that thar's one o' them outlaws! Maybe he knows we're here!"

Hildy didn't answer, but watched anxiously as the flashlight's beam passed the trucks and the powerful-looking Cadillac with its gleaming hood ornament.

Only the man's legs and hands could be seen as they moved in and out of the shaft of light. Whoever the man was, he apparently didn't want to be seen any more than Hildy and Ruby did.

Hildy realized she was holding her breath, and her heart thumped so hard her ribs hurt. She watched anxiously as the man crawled over the manger on the far side of the barn.

He's coming this way! Hildy's mind screamed. She was tempted to make a desperate effort to get away, but knew it would be impossible without making any noise.

Then a thought exploded in Hildy's brain, *Where's Mischief?*

Desperate, Hildy looked around, but couldn't see anything. She reached out, groping for her pet, but couldn't feel or hear her.

The man left the manger and directed the flashlight beam along the straw. Then Hildy spotted Mischief in the soft glow at the edge of the light. She was heading straight toward the man, moving as fast as her rolling gait would permit.

"Lookee yonder!" Ruby whispered. "She's a-goin' straight to 'im!"

Hildy's heart leaped. She debated what to do.

Suddenly the man stopped. His flashlight focused on the pile of gunnysacks.

Mischief also stopped. Hildy swallowed hard as the dark figure bent down and began pulling the sacks aside. He picked up a gun.

Hildy gulped, recognizing it from newspaper pictures as a Thompson submachine gun or "tommy gun," favored by criminals.

If he sees me—Hildy thought with rising terror.

She held her breath as the man gently laid the gun on the sacks he had pulled aside. Still securing the flashlight in one hand, he dug deeper into the remaining sacks.

Hildy didn't move. She prayed silently that Mischief would remain still and not be seen.

Then Hildy saw the man lift a burlap-covered jug from under the pile. He pulled the cork and pressed his nose close to smell the contents. He skillfully hooked his right forefinger through the small handle, swung the jug up to rest on his right forearm, and took a drink.

Hildy heard the screen door on the house creak open again.

"Jiggs?" It was the voice of Dixie Mae's father. "Where are you?"

The flashlight went out, but in the instant before it did, Hildy saw Mischief starting toward the man again.

Oh, no! she thought.

"Answer me, Jiggs!" the call came again. "Are you out in the barn?"

The man didn't answer. Hildy heard him moving about quickly and guessed he was hiding the jug. At the same time, she heard the screen door slam. Through the far barn door where the first man had entered, a lantern revealed Dixie Mae's father heading for the barn.

He's coming this way! Hildy thought in panic. *What'll we do?*

Obviously hearing something in the dark barn, Jiggs turned on the flashlight again. He swept the interior with it, then focused on Mischief.

"What the—?" Seeing the approaching animal in his light, the man lurched backward.

"Mad coon!" he yelled, stumbling awkwardly toward the manger. "Mad coo—"

His second cry broke off as the man backed against the manger and fell over it to the ground. The flashlight sailed crazily through the air, making whirling shadows against the walls and ceiling. It landed with a loud crack and the light went out.

Hux Stonecipher's lantern appeared in the open barn door. "What're you yelling about?" he demanded, holding the light high.

Hildy saw the frightened man desperately scramble to his feet. He ran toward the lantern, shouting and pointing behind him. "There's a mad raccoon after me! Look out, it'll bite us both!"

"Where?" Hux asked, holding the light even higher and moving it back and forth.

"He ran toward the other side of the barn!" Jiggs yelled.

Hildy was as tense as a banjo string at a hoedown from fear

for herself, Ruby, and Mischief. She saw with relief that the little animal was retreating toward her, apparently frightened by Jiggs' fall and all the yelling. Seconds later, Mischief raced into Hildy's arms.

"Quick!" she whispered, shoving her pet through the window to Ruby. "Take her!"

Ruby hastily complied, and Hildy reached up to climb through the window just as Jiggs yelled, "Gimme that lantern! I'll grab the tommy gun and blast that coon to pieces!"

CHAPTER NINE

A CLUE

Late Wednesday Night

Hildy frantically felt for the open barn window while one wild thought crossed her mind: *If he starts firing that machine gun, he'll hit us all!*

The outline of the window could be seen faintly in the light of the distant lantern. Ruby's face was barely discernible as she tried to secure the squirming coon.

Hildy swung one leg through the window opening and glanced back. The lantern, held high, gave her a quick glimpse of Dixie Mae's father.

"Jiggs," he shouted angrily, "let go of my lantern! Phew! Your breath stinks! Get away from me!"

"But, Hux, that coon—"

"In your condition you wouldn't know a coon from a grizzly bear! Get inside and sober up! You've got to be ready to hit that train Friday. Now, move!"

Hildy saw Dixie Mae's father kick the man he called Jiggs, sending him stumbling through the open barn door into the darkness. Hux followed after him with the lantern. The heavy door slid shut, and the interior of the barn went black.

Hildy hastily slipped through the window. When she touched ground, she whispered to Ruby, "Did you hear what he just said about robbing the train on Friday?"

"Shore 'nuf! We gotta tell yore daddy an' Ben."

Mischief complained with piteous little cries as Hildy ran with her through the fields, and the cousins arrived breathlessly at the Corrigan's tar-paper shack.

"Daddy! Brother Ben!" Hildy cried, running into the living room. "Guess what? Those outlaws—"

"Where's the girl?" her father interrupted.

"She couldn't come," Hildy answered. "Maybe tomorrow night. But we heard that the gang's planning to rob the gold train on Friday!"

The girls hurriedly recounted all that had happened.

When they finished, Hildy's father scolded, "Neither of you should have gone over there without telling us. You could have been hurt!"

"I'm sorry, Daddy. I didn't think there was time. We'd already waited so long for Dixie Mae in our barn. But we're safe now. Let's talk about what to do next."

"Yeah!" Ruby exclaimed. "We cain't he'p Dixie Mae until tomorry night, an' them outlaws are gonna rob the train sometime the followin' day!"

The two men exchanged glances, and the old ranger reached for his big white hat. "Let's all go talk to Matt Farnham. His gold is carried on that train."

They all piled into the Packard and stopped at a pay phone outside Lone River to call the banker. After the call, the old ranger returned to the car and announced that Matt Farnham would unlock the gate to his estate and be waiting up. Hildy wondered if Spud would be there too.

When they reached the Farnhams, Joe Corrigan got out and swung open the right half of the gate to the driveway. A dog barked sharply, and Hildy saw an Airedale come bounding down the front steps of the three-story frame mansion. He raced toward them, as if to challenge the intruders.

"Lindy!" Spud's stern voice could be heard from inside the screened-in back porch, which ran the length of the mansion's north side. "Quiet! It's okay!"

Hildy smiled to herself, but Ruby grumbled under her breath. "I shoulda knowed Spud'd be thar!"

"Please try to be more tolerant of him," Hildy pleaded. Spud's hair was rumpled, and Hildy guessed he'd been asleep when the old ranger phoned the house.

"Greetings and felicitations!" the ruddy-faced boy said with a grin as the group got out of the car. "Uncle Matt's waiting for you upstairs."

"Upstairs?" Hildy asked in surprise. She wondered why he wasn't waiting in the usual downstairs parlor, but didn't ask.

Ruby mimicked Spud under her breath. "Greetin's and sich like. Greetin's an—"

"Ruby!" Hildy hissed. "He'll hear you!"

"I don't keer! He makes me so blasted mad with his hifalutin big words! Thinks he's so smart!"

Hildy gripped her cousin's arm. "Please! There are too many important things to talk about tonight."

Ruby didn't respond, but was politely silent as Spud led them across the porch and through the rich mahogany door with a frosted-glass window. Their footsteps were muted by the intricate Persian rug in the entryway. They followed Spud up the stairs.

At the top, he turned to the right down the long carpeted hallway, where a single small bulb in a green shade provided the only light. "Aunt Beryl and the kids are asleep downstairs. Uncle Matt says we can talk better up here."

Because she worked in the house, Hildy was familiar with the upstairs hallway. There were six bedroom doors, three on each side. When the banker's wife was stricken with polio and confined to a wheelchair, new bedrooms were added downstairs.

Hildy was acquainted with two of the upstairs rooms because the Farnham children, Dickie and Connie, sometimes liked to play in their old bedrooms. But she had never been inside the last room on the left, which was always locked.

When Spud paused at the door, Hildy blinked in surprise and looked at Ruby. "Did you hear that?"

"Shore did! Sounds like a train whistle!"

Spud smiled and opened the door.

The room was completely dark except for a tiny white light that moved along the far wall. Spud twisted the light switch by the door, and the room was illuminated by a single bulb and glass reflector suspended on a braided cord that hung from the ceiling.

Hildy saw then that the tiny lamp was the headlight on a toy electric locomotive. The whistle on the engine sounded again as it carried the four miniature cars down the long track.

Matt Farnham looked up and smiled as he brought the train to a halt. "Model railroading's my hobby," he explained somewhat sheepishly.

Hildy had seen pictures of electric and wind-up trains in a mail-order catalog. They ran on an oval track just three feet around. But this model railroad had a set of tracks that had been built on a shelf about chest high. It stretched along three sides of the room, a distance of about sixty feet.

The terrain had been scaled to size, with mountains about two feet high, trees, brush, river trestles, dry gulches, and a few buildings. There were even some deer and a bear.

Mr. Farnham told them, "This track is a reproduction of the narrow-gauge rail line that runs between the hard-rock gold mines at Quartz City to where the line connects with the standard-gauge trains at Colfax."

The old ranger nodded. "And you were studying it to see where the bandits plan to stage the holdup I called about."

"At the tunnel!" Hildy exclaimed, her eyes sweeping the long track. "There!" She pointed to the left. "Isn't that a tunnel?"

The banker nodded. "Yes, it is."

Ruby cried, "That's whar them outlaws is a-gonna try to rob ye come Friday! All ye got to do is git the po-lice to grab 'em when they show up."

Spud chuckled. "How do you know that's the tunnel?" He pointed to the left. "There are two more over there." He turned to the right. "And two more on this side. Now, which of the five is going to be attacked?"

Hildy sensed that Ruby was stiffening and about to make an angry reply. "Because trains run on a schedule," Hildy quickly spoke up, "couldn't you check to see what time the train arrives at each tunnel?"

The banker shook his head. "It's true that trains generally run on a schedule, but not this one. It goes when it has a load, and that could be any time of the day or night, seven days a week."

Ruby appeared to defend their mistake about the tunnel. "Dixie Mae's daddy said it's gonna be Friday. How could them thar outlaws be a-plannin' to rob it 'lessen they knowed when it was a-gonna run?"

The old ranger gave his moustache a flip with the back of his right forefinger. "I think she's got you there, Matt."

"Good question, Ruby," the banker said with a faint smile. "You'd think one of the best-kept secrets in the world would be when a gold train's going to make a run. But it's not."

Hildy walked to the left, at the start of the model railroad track. A tiny sign on the depot read QUARTZ CITY. She walked slowly along the track, taking notice of the various tunnels. They were all marked with signs: MOUNT OSO, COPPER MOUNTAIN, DEVIL'S PEAK, SHAW'S SUMMIT, and LOBO RIDGE. The line ended at another depot labeled COLFAX.

Ben Strong commented, "The reason it's not a secret is because people are creatures of habit. I've spent enough time up in that area to know that the trainmen who make up the cars for a gold shipment always do it in the same way."

"That's right." Hildy's father spoke for the first time. "When I was up there recently, I heard that even the hoboes who live along the track can tell when a shipment is about to be sent from the mines to Colfax."

"So," Hildy said, studying the fifth and last tunnel, "the bandits must have someone watching the railroad. Whoever it is must have let Dixie Mae's father know that a train was being loaded the way it is when the owners are going to ship gold."

"You've got it," the banker replied. "But even I didn't know a shipment was planned for this Friday."

Ruby asked, "Ye gonna have yore gold on that train?"

"My mine always has a shipment. Sometimes it's not very much, sometimes it's a lot. No matter how much it is, I can't afford to lose it. But I'm wondering how we can prevent the attack if we don't know which tunnel Stonecipher and his gang plan to hit?"

"Why not put policemen at all five tunnels?" Hildy suggested, retracing her steps along the miniature track.

"That would spread the law-enforcement officials too thin," the ranger explained. "Even if they called in outside assistance, it may not be enough. And if that many officers were seen, whoever's spying on the train would surely notice the unusual activity and call off the attack."

"That'd be good, wouldn't it?" Ruby asked.

"Temporarily," the banker replied, "but it would leave them free to try again another day when we might not be prepared. We've got to figure out a way to prevent the robbery and capture the gang, too."

Hildy glanced at the five tunnels again and said, "I think I have an idea that might work."

"You have?" Spud asked, moving to her side. "What is it?"

Hildy hesitated, fearful of saying something foolish. She glanced uncertainly at her father, knowing that if the old ranger and the banker hadn't figured it out, her chances of doing so were slim.

Her father prompted, "Tell us."

Hildy asked, "How exact to scale is this model?"

"Very exact," the banker said with obvious pride. "Every feature of the terrain duplicates what's on the actual short line. Why?"

"Well," Hildy said, "there are no roads crossing the tracks

anywhere near the first two tunnels." She pointed. "See?"

"That's right," the banker agreed. "So what are you suggesting?"

"There are roads near the other three tunnels, but only one has a road real close. This one." Hildy gingerly touched the sand on what was to represent an unpaved rural road. On it were a miniature hay wagon, a touring car, and a horse and buggy. "The one marked SHAW'S SUMMIT."

The banker's eyes lit up. "Of course!" he exclaimed. "That road crosses the tracks at the south end of the Shaw's Summit tunnel, just before the rails start the steep downhill grade to Dead Man's Curve. Hildy, I think you've got it!" He turned to Ben. "What do you think?"

"I agree! Now, why didn't I think of that?"

Hildy's father snapped his fingers. "The trucks you girls saw in the barn—the outlaws must be planning to use them to haul the gold away from the railroad along that road. But which way will they go?"

Ben asked, "Matt, do you know where this road leads?"

"At Shaw's Summit crossing, it goes east toward Reno, Nevada, and west toward Sacramento."

"I figure they're planning to grab the gold from the railroad, put it on trucks and drive off. They have to stay on good roads because the gold is heavy," the old ranger mused, "but they wouldn't dare risk being on any road for very long."

"Of course," Spud agreed, "word would be out about the robbery. The police would have set up roadblocks to check suspicious trucks. So what *are* they going to do with the stolen bullion?"

The old ranger lightly stroked his moustache. "They could go a short distance, hide the gold, and come back for it later. Or, they could switch it from the trucks to other vehicles that the police won't be looking for."

"But if they do that, couldn't they get away with the gold?" Hildy asked.

The old ranger nodded. "They sure could. That's why we

have to try to prevent the robbery from taking place. Thanks to you girls, we know where and roughly when they plan to attack. What we don't have, is much time to figure out how to stop it and catch the gang."

A long discussion followed, but nothing was resolved. At last the old ranger lightly tapped a forefinger on the miniature tunnel marked SHAW'S SUMMIT. "I'd better get up there tomorrow and see what we're up against. Now, we'd better all get some sleep."

Ben took Ruby home to her father's place. Hildy was so excited she didn't want to go home, but when she and her father stepped into their tar-paper shack, Hildy realized how weary she was. It was lonely and quiet without the rest of the Corrigan family.

Hildy went to the dining room window. She stood looking thoughtfully toward the distant ranch house where Dixie Mae was held prisoner by her own outlaw father.

Suddenly Hildy tensed, and placed both hands against the cold windowpane to shut out the light from the lamp behind her.

"Dad!" she called. "Come quick! I can see lights from the outlaws' trucks and car! They're leaving!" Panic washed over her. "And they must be taking Dixie Mae with them!"

Chapter Ten

THREE MYSTERIOUS WORDS

Early Thursday Morning

Hildy awakened at daybreak in the quiet house. She slid out from under the warm covers in the unheated room. She threw an old quilt over her shoulders and padded barefoot across the cold linoleum floor.

Mischief followed, playfully tugging at the trailing end of the quilt. Hildy entered the kitchen where her father had lit the kerosene lamp and was laying a fire.

Hildy's long hair, unbraided, flowed freely about her face. "Daddy," she began, "I've been thinking about that gang leaving last night. Do you think they came back after we went to sleep?"

"I doubt it." Joe struck a wooden match on the stovetop and touched the flame to the paper and kindling he had laid in the firebox.

"Then where did they go—and why?"

"Probably closer to where they plan to rob the train—for convenience, and maybe because there's no stove in that house for cooking or heating, and winter's coming fast."

"I thought of that, too. If Dixie Mae knew where they were going, she may have left a clue—figuring I'd come looking in the old house. That would be the only way we could find her and help her get back to her mother. Could we go over there and have a look around?"

"I suppose so."

"When?"

"Right after breakfast. You know, there's another reason why the gang may have pulled out last night, and the thought of it scares me. Suppose the girl told them about you and Ruby, and what we all planned to do?"

"Dixie Mae wouldn't have done that. We're trying to help her!" Hildy protested.

"Maybe she wouldn't have said anything willingly. But you told us you thought her father had hit her. If her father was suspicious because she was slow coming to the house when he called her, he could have threatened to hurt her unless she told what she was doing in the barn."

"Oh, Daddy, she wouldn't!"

"She might have if she were frightened enough. And if she told, the outlaws had only two choices: to run and hide again, or—" His voice trailed off.

"Or what?" Hildy prompted, sensing her father's reluctance to say what he thought.

"Or to make sure you and Ruby don't tell anyone."

Hildy sucked in her breath. "Do you think the gang would do something to us?"

"I don't want to scare you, but it's possible."

Hildy frowned, thinking fast. "Dixie Mae knew Ruby and I were going to need some grown-ups to help—you and Brother Ben and Molly. That means, instead of the bandits going after just Ruby and me, our whole family could be in danger!"

"That occurred to me. I think you and Ruby should join the rest of the family and stay away until that gang's behind bars. Ben's place should be safe."

"You mean we wouldn't even go to school?"

"When this is all over, I'll explain everything to your principal, and to Elizabeth's and Martha's, too. All your grades are good enough that you could make up a few days of school without much trouble."

"How about Ruby?"

"What she does is up to Nate. I'll tell him right after we talk to Ben."

"He planned to go to the foothills today, but I hope he's still home so we can tell him that the gang's gone—with Dixie Mae."

"If he's left already, we can phone Matt Farnham. He'll know how to reach Ben in the gold country."

"If Ben hasn't left, may I ride up with him?"

"I don't want you out of my sight until this thing's settled, Hildy. Right after breakfast we'll go over and check out that place next door. Once we know for sure the gang's gone, we'll drive over to Ben's. We can see how your mother and your sisters and brother are doing."

Half an hour later Hildy and her father bundled up against the chill and drove to the old house next door. Hildy noticed that the window coverings had been removed. The window-panes seemed to stare again like dead, empty eyes. The front door stood open, as did the sliding barn door. Even from a distance, Hildy could see that the three trucks and the Cadillac were gone.

"No sign of anybody around," her father said quietly, standing in the open area between the barn and house. He and Hildy stepped warily to the open front door. He called, "Anybody home?" There was no answer.

They quickly searched the downstairs. It was chilly, and for Hildy, a little scary. She noticed the floor was littered with cheap crime novels, cigarette butts, and other trash. There was the smell of kerosene, as though they'd tried to heat the big place with a small portable stove.

The two climbed the steps to the second story. There were four bedrooms, two on each side of the short hall. The first three rooms they checked were empty except for some old newspapers, an empty tobacco sack, and other debris.

As her father lingered to check the closet in one of the three rooms, Hildy moved to the last bedroom. She saw some lined paper scattered on the wooden floor, and then Hildy spotted the royal blue beret.

This was Dixie Mae's room, she thought. She started to pick up the hat, then changed her mind. *It would just make me sad to have something to remind me of her,* Hildy told herself. *I'll just check the papers to see if she left a note.*

Hildy looked on both sides of every lined sheet of paper. It appeared that Dixie Mae had simply practiced her penmanship on them. There was no note, no hint as to where Dixie Mae had been taken.

Hildy's father entered the room. "I didn't find anything that would be of help in locating them."

"Oh, Daddy!" Hildy cried in a sad voice, "I feel like I've let Dixie Mae down. I told her I'd help her tonight to get back to her mother. Now she's gone, and we don't know where."

"Remember, she could have come with you last night when she had the chance, Hildy. Let's go to Ben's place, then Nate's." Joe bent to pick up the blue beret. "I wonder why she left this?"

"She probably left in such a hurry that she dropped it."

As Hildy's father stood up, the beret in his hand, a piece of paper fluttered to the floor.

Hildy could make out one word on the paper: *Hildy*. She quickly stooped to recover the note. Three other words followed her name: *Twin Pines School.*

"What do you suppose this means, Daddy?" Hildy asked, turning to show him.

He studied the words for a moment, then shrugged. "If it didn't have your name on it, I'd say it didn't mean anything. But since it does, Dixie Mae must have been trying to tell you something. Did she mention the school last night?"

"No, and I don't know of any school by that name. But I'm sure Dixie Mae was trying to leave a clue. Let's see—" Hildy took a couple of quick steps, thinking fast. "She must have figured

I'd come over here. And she knows she'll never get back to her mother unless somebody helps her. That's us. So she left her beret with—I've got it!"

Her father glanced quizzically at her. "What do you mean?"

"They must have taken her up to the foothills so they could get ready to rob the train. They've probably got a hideout somewhere near the railroad. Maybe we could find her up there before the robbery takes place."

"That railroad runs for about twenty miles."

"It's the only lead we've got! If Brother Ben's still home, I could ride up with him."

"Try to be reasonable, Hildy. Even if I did let you go, where would you even begin looking for the girl?"

"Remember the railroad tunnel that Dixie Mae mentioned to Ruby and me last night—the place where the train's supposed to be robbed?"

"Yes, but what's that got to do with finding her?"

"Somebody from the gang might be watching that tunnel. If I could be there and follow that person back to their new hideout—"

"Whoa, now! You could get caught."

"I'd be careful, Daddy."

"How could a girl like you—alone—be of any help in finding Dixie Mae?"

"I wouldn't be alone. Brother Ben would be with me. And I just thought of something else—only Ruby and I know what Dixie Mae looks like. And only Ruby and I saw her father. Maybe Ruby could go up, too."

"Hux Stonecipher's picture has been in the papers lots of times."

"But what about Jiggs, the outlaw who wanted to shoot Mischief? His picture may never have been printed, but I could watch—"

"Listen, Hildy!" her father interrupted. "I'm just glad those people are out of here, and that our family is safe. I'd like to help the girl, but we're not going to risk your life doing it."

"If Dixie Mae's father and his men do rob the train, they'll immediately leave for parts unknown," Hildy protested. "No one may ever see Dixie Mae again. She's got to be found and helped to escape before then. I promised, Daddy!"

"I'm sorry, Hildy. You've already done what you could for the girl. Now, let's go to Ben's place."

Hildy fought back a sick feeling inside, knowing that she and Dixie Mae were racing against the clock, and both were losing. As she rode beside her father in the Rickenbacker, Hildy desperately tried again:

"I know how we can find out if Twin Pines School is near the railroad! Mr. Farnham said that his miniature railroad is an exact model of everything between Quartz City and Colfax. Maybe there's a model of a schoolhouse that we missed. Mr. Farnham would know if it's called Twin Pines. I need to talk to him."

"When we get to Ben's house, you can use his phone to call Matt. He probably hasn't gone to the bank yet."

Ben Strong's home was a low, rambling frame house set well off the road and near a small creek. Eucalyptus and cottonwood trees sheltered the house, barn, and corrals. There were no animals in sight, although Hildy knew Ben had an old horse.

As Joe stopped the Rickenbacker, Hildy's four little sisters came running out. Molly followed, carrying Joey.

Hildy was happy to see that her little brother was well. Molly said he hadn't had any more signs of ear problems. She was visibly relieved when told that the outlaws had left last night, but expressed her sadness that Dixie Mae was gone, too.

Hildy asked about Brother Ben and learned that he had talked to Matt Farnham on the phone a little while ago, and had then gone to see the banker at his home.

Hildy used the old ranger's phone to call the Farnham home. The banker answered. Hildy was happy to learn that Ben was still there. To save time, she asked Mr. Farnham to pass on to Brother Ben what she would tell him. First she told about the bandits leaving, and then the mysterious note Dixie Mae had left, with the words *Twin Pines School.*

Mr. Farnham said, "I know that name. It's a one-room country school that you may have seen on my miniature railroad model."

"I don't remember the school," Hildy answered. "Where is it?"

"At the bottom of the grade coming down from Shaw's Summit tunnel, right at Dead Man's Curve."

"Is the school still in use?"

"Yes. Why?"

"Oh, I thought it might be empty, and that the outlaws could be using it as another hideout." Hildy swallowed her disappointment and added, "Please tell Brother Ben, and see if he has any ideas as to what the note could mean."

Hildy said goodbye, replaced the earpiece on the hook, and looked at her family.

Her father said, "I've just explained everything to Molly. She agrees with me that the family should stay away from our place until we're sure it's safe. Because Ben's going to the foothills, we can remain here awhile.

"Hildy, let's go tell Nate and Ruby what's happened so far. We can stop by our place on the way. You can check on your raccoon while I grab a few jars of salmon. I'll give Mrs. Radcliffe the fish when Molly and I go to have Joey's ear checked."

Hildy nodded and bent to kiss Joey. He stood, grasping a chair made of bristly red and white cowhide.

"You stay well," she said, pressing her cheek against his cool face.

"Bye-bye," he said, opening and closing his little palm in a wave.

"Bye, Joey. See you later. Bye, everybody. Daddy and I will be back shortly."

As Hildy and her father approached the front porch of their home, Hildy stopped abruptly. "The door's open!"

She ran ahead of her father. "It's been pried open!" she exclaimed. "The lock's broken!"

When she pushed on the door, a piece of paper fluttered to the ground. Hildy snatched it up. The words seemed to leap at her.

This is what you get for sticking your nose in where it don't belong.

Chapter Eleven

A HARD DECISION

Thursday Morning

Hildy quickly reread the note. There was no signature. She looked anxiously at her father, then at the broken lock. He opened the door, stepped inside the screened-in front porch and stopped with a groan.

Hildy stepped up beside him and cried in dismay, "Oh, Daddy, they've wrecked everything!"

Her little sisters' bedding was dumped on the floor. In the living room, the hickory rocker had been tipped on its side and the couch slashed so that the stuffing stuck out of gaping holes.

Joe Corrigan stormed through the rest of the small house, trailing strong words Hildy had never heard before. She followed him, feeling sick to her stomach.

The handcrafted dining room table had been overturned and one leg was missing. The base of the coal-oil lamp was gone, and the chimney lay shattered on the floor.

Hildy carefully picked her way through the broken glass to her bedroom door. "Oh, no!" she gasped, closing her eyes. Her and Elizabeth's cots had been overturned and trampled. The bedding was in a heap on the floor, and large, dirty footprints could be seen on the girls' few pieces of clothing, which were also scattered on the floor.

Her father's call from the kitchen brought Hildy dashing to his side. She stopped short at the sight of the mess in the middle of the floor. A hundred-pound sack of potatoes, fifty pounds of red beans, and the flour bin had all been dumped together. Kerosene from the lamps had been splashed over everything.

Hildy wrinkled her nose at the strong odor of fuel and fish. She glanced inside the cupboard. Shards of glass jars glinted amid the slashed salmon on the floor.

Joe Corrigan muttered in disbelief, "They broke every jar with the table leg!" His face revealed his anger. "Everything is ruined!" he said, his voice cracking. "There's not a thing we can use."

"Oh, Daddy, I can't believe anyone would be so mean! How will we live through this winter?"

"I don't know, but I do know this means the girl told her father about meeting with you and Ruby."

"Her daddy must have scared her plenty to make her tell about us," Hildy said in defense of Dixie Mae.

Joe took a slow, deep breath, then said quietly, "We can't leave this kerosene-soaked mess. If a match touched it, we'd lose what little bit we have left. I'll find some lug boxes. You get the shovels."

Hildy nodded, starting for the back door. She stopped abruptly. "Mischief! I haven't seen her."

"She's probably hiding in the barn someplace. Take a look around when you get the shovels."

Hildy dashed out the back door and raced toward the barn, calling for her pet. *If they hurt Mischief!* Hildy told herself fiercely, *I'll—I'll—*. Her thought was unfinished as she saw Mischief waddle out of the barn.

Hildy bent to pick up her pet, speaking soothing words while examining the animal to be sure she was uninjured. Satisfied that she was fine, Hildy lifted Mischief to her favorite perch on her neck, grabbed the two shovels, and returned to the house.

Hildy helped her father shovel the beans, potatoes, flour, and fish into wooden lug boxes. Then he carried them out behind the barn to be buried later.

When he returned, Hildy picked up Mischief and followed her father to the car. As they turned for a last look at their home, Hildy cried, "Oh, Daddy, what will we do so we don't starve?"

"I'll think of something. This makes me mad!" he said through gritted teeth. "We're not going to be scared off. I'm going to help you find that girl and see that her father and his gang go to jail."

The two drove directly to the nearby ranch where Ruby and her father lived in the bunkhouse behind the main house. The bunkhouse was built in the days when many riders were needed on the ranch.

Ruby was coming down the driveway with her lunch pail as the Rickenbacker pulled up. "What on earth brings ye two out this-away so early?" she asked, peering in at Hildy.

"Is your father home?" Hildy's father asked bruskly, sliding out of the driver's seat.

Ruby nodded. "He's a-workin' on his sermon. I was jist a-gonna ketch the school bus."

"Come back inside with us, Ruby," Hildy's father said grimly. "What I have to say to your father concerns you too."

The front door opened and Nate Konning looked out. "I thought I heard your voice, Joe," he said with a smile. Then it vanished. "Oh-oh, trouble?" he asked.

"Lots of it, Nate," Hildy's father said, stepping through the doorway.

The bunkhouse where the Konnings lived consisted of one long room with rows of bunkbeds lining two walls. Blankets suspended from baling wire created two private sleeping areas for Nate and Ruby.

The interior walls and ceiling had been finished by nailing old cardboard cartons to the two-by-fours. There was a small table with a kerosene lamp on it, two ancient straight-back chairs, an old wood-burning kitchen stove that also heated the room, and some lug boxes.

Hildy was fairly bursting to tell Ruby all that had happened, but knew she would have to wait until her father had finished speaking. When he was upset about something, he didn't like to be interrupted. He took one of the two chairs, and Ruby's father sat down on the other. The cousins pulled up empty lug boxes for seats.

Hildy waited until her father had related everything that had happened, including the vandalism at their home.

When he was quiet, Hildy said, "So, Ruby, Daddy thinks you and I might be in danger, as well as our families. Uncle Nate, you should go with us to Brother Ben's until the crooks are caught."

The tall lanky preacher pondered her words a moment in silence.

Ruby stood, then walked to the far end of the room, beckoning Hildy to follow. At the window, Ruby lowered her voice. "Are ye skeered?"

"I'm so upset with those awful men for what they did that I haven't had time to think about being scared."

"Ye'll be safe at Ben's. But what are ye gonna do while yo're stayin' thar?"

"Daddy says he's going to help us find Dixie Mae."

"Don't say us! After she done tol' on us and got yore house wrecked, I ain't a-gonna he'p find her!"

"But we promised!"

"Ye done the promisin', Hildy! Far's I'm concerned, she don't deserve nobody to keer a bean about her now."

"You know she wouldn't have told on us unless she was forced to!"

"I don't keer! Nobody could whop me so hard that I'd tell on somebody who's a-tryin' to he'p me!"

Hildy realized it was useless to try reasoning further with her cousin, so she changed the subject. "Let's go see what Uncle Nate's decided about you going with us to Brother Ben's."

"Even if'n he makes me go, I'm a-telling ye flat out that I ain't a-gonna he'p ye find that Dixie Mae!"

Hildy started back to where her father and uncle were talking in low tones. She said to Ruby, "Soon's we get back to Brother Ben's, I'll phone Mr. Farnham and see if Brother Ben is still there. If he is, maybe I can ride up to the foothills with him."

The men looked up as Hildy and Ruby returned. Joe stood. "Hildy, we overlooked something," he began. "We can't go off and leave Molly right now, not when Joey might have another spell."

"What are you going to do?" Hildy asked, suddenly feeling caught between two difficult choices. She didn't want to leave her little brother, either, yet she had promised to help Dixie Mae, and that meant going to look for her in the foothills.

"I'll figure that out on the way to Ben's," Hildy's father replied. "Nate, you're sure you're going to stick with your decision?"

He nodded. "Ruby, honey, grab a suitcase and throw some of your things into it. I think you'll be safer at Ben's until those outlaws are caught."

"Ain't ye a-comin' too?" Ruby asked.

"There's no reason to be concerned about me. But now that Hux Stonecipher knows about you and Hildy, he might have some of his gang watch for you when you're alone—at school, or waiting for the bus. Joe and I want to avoid that possibility. You go ahead now while I finish my sermon." He stood to put his arms around Ruby. "One more thing," he said softly. "Don't let Hildy out of your sight until this is over."

Hildy's father added, "Same goes for you, Hildy. Stay with Ruby. You'll both be safer, and Nate and I can rest easier."

As they drove away from the Konning place, Hildy asked Ruby, "Do you remember those nice people we met up at the mines last month?"

"Shore do! There was that thar miner's boy, Jack Tremayne, and that strange old man who called hisself Skeezix. I shore would admire to see them ag'in."

"Me too!" Hildy glanced at her father. "Maybe they can help us find Dixie Mae."

"Just hold your horses, Hildy," her father said. "I haven't decided yet if we can let you go up there right now."

"But you said you wanted us to find Dixie Mae and see her father and his gang put in prison."

"I meant that, but your trip may have to wait."

"Daddy, the robbery's going to take place tomorrow! If Dixie Mae's not found before then, the outlaws will run off and I'll never see her again."

Ruby surprised Hildy by saying, "Her an' me might be safer up in the foothills with Ben than down here. Maybe the men who wrecked yore place are a-lookin' fer us around here."

Hildy noticed a slight blush on her cousin's cheeks. She guessed that Ruby's real reason for wanting to go to the mines was to see Jack Tremayne again.

Hildy's father said, "I'll talk to Molly first, then Ben and Matt. Then I'll make a decision."

At the old ranger's house, Molly reported that Joey was still doing fine. Hildy picked up the phone and started to ask the operator to get her Matt Farnham's home just as Ruby called, "Here comes Ben!"

Hildy replaced the receiver and joined the others gathered at the back door. When the old ranger stopped the Packard, Elizabeth and Martha led the younger sisters in, reporting to him their excited though secondhand report of the mess the bandits had left at their house.

The little girls were quiet when their father took over, filling in the details. "So," he concluded, "I decided to take you up on your invitation for us to stay here a few days until those crooks are caught. Nate sent Ruby along too. Hope you don't mind."

"I'm glad to have all of you," Ben said. "I guess it's a good thing I forgot my razor and had to come back for it. We'd better talk about this some more before I start up for the hills again."

All six of the girls followed Joe Corrigan, Ben, and Molly into the living room. But only Hildy and Ruby were allowed to stay and join the adults in discussion of the situation because it directly involved the two older girls.

At first it was exciting to Hildy to have a part in the conversation, but her enthusiasm gradually wore off. She glanced at Ruby, who suppressed a bored yawn.

Because the final decision would not be Hildy's or Ruby's, they quietly left the adults and slipped into the kitchen.

Hildy asked, "Are you mad at me because our fathers said we have to stick together?"

"It warn't yore fault they said that."

"Then if Daddy decides I can go with Brother Ben to look for Dixie Mae, you won't mind going along?"

"Like I said, I figger we don't owe her nothin' now, on accounta her tellin' on us so's yore house got ruined. But you'n me is friends, an' that ain't a-gonna change nohow."

"Thanks," Hildy said with a warm smile, then added with a teasing grin, "Maybe Jack Tremayne can help us find Dixie Mae."

Ruby looked flustered and quickly changed the subject. She glanced toward the living room, where they could still hear the adults talking. "What do ye reckon they's gonna decide?"

"It's hard to say. There are so many things to think about. I know Daddy and I can't both go off and leave Molly with all the kids in a strange house, especially when Joey might need an operation.

"But I promised to help Dixie Mae. In fact, I told her that all things are possible to those who believe, and she said she liked that."

"I remember."

Hildy sighed, sadly shaking her head. "But it's sure hard to know what to do in this situation."

"I reckon muh daddy'll tell his congregation what happened, and folks'll see that ye git new bedding and some food an' sich like."

"That would be kind of them, but Daddy's so proud I'm not sure he'd accept—" She broke off suddenly. "Daddy's calling!"

Hildy and Ruby hurried into the living room and stopped as all three adults looked up at them.

Joe Corrigan cleared his throat. "We've made a decision

about whether you girls should go with Ben to look for Dixie Mae."

Hildy held her breath, anxious to hear what had been decided.

———

FOLLOW THAT CAR!

Thursday Afternoon

An hour later, Hildy, Ruby, and the old ranger were on their way to the gold country. Hildy's father had decided to let them go, but thought it better that he stay with Molly in case Joey became ill again.

Ben Strong turned his gaze from the highway to the girls, who were sitting beside him in the big Packard. "We should be there in about four hours."

Ruby asked, "Do ye reckon we'll see Jack Tremayne?"

"I wouldn't be surprised," Ben replied. "After the way he helped us last month when we were up here, he'd be a good one to assist us now."

Hildy smiled, recalling the miner's son. Then she felt a little sadness that Spud wasn't with them. Aloud, she asked, "Brother Ben, what about Skeezix?"

"We'll look him up too. I figure that anyone who hangs around the railroad as much as he does could help us solve this case. But I sure wish Spud were with us."

"Me too," Hildy said, but Ruby made a snorting noise that plainly said where she stood when it came to Spud.

"We'd better talk over some ideas of how best to accomplish what we're going up here to do," Ben suggested. "We can start by making sure our goals are clear."

"That thar's plumb easy!" Ruby replied. "We got to keep them bad men from stealin' the gold off'n that little ol' train."

Hildy added quickly, "But we've got to find Dixie Mae first, and help her return to her mother. I promised that."

"We need to do both those things," the old ranger agreed, "but those outlaws must be caught with enough evidence to put them in prison. Otherwise, you girls and your families and homes might still be at risk."

"We would still be in danger," Hildy agreed, thinking of the terrible mess the outlaws had made of their meager possessions at the tar-paper shack, "but so would Dixie Mae, even if—I mean, *when*—we find her, because her father could kidnap her again if he doesn't end up in jail for a long, long time."

"So," the old ranger continued, "we have our goals clearly in mind. Now let's think of ways to reach them."

Hildy mentioned the note Dixie Mae had left with the words *Twin Pines School*, and the fact that Matt Farnham had told them where the school was located. The search could begin around there.

Ben mentioned the police informant at Quartz City, who might have some information, and Ruby suggested that Skeezix or Jack may know of possible hiding places where the outlaws would be close to the railroad, yet out of sight until the time of the attack.

Ruby commented, "Don't forgit the tunnel at Shaw's Summit, an' the robbery planned for tomorrow. Too bad we don't know the exact time them badmen plan to try robbin' the train."

"We could drive by both the school and the tunnel on our way to Quartz City," the old ranger suggested. "Right now, I'd better stop at the next filling station. This big engine will use a lot of gas climbing those hills."

At the base of the foothills, Ben pulled the Packard into a combination gas station and cafe. Hildy noticed two small signs next to the two gas pumps. One read: FLATS FIXED. FREE WATER AND AIR. The second read: HOT HOME-COOKED LUNCHES, 35 CENTS.

"You girls hungry?" the old ranger asked as he maneuvered the car alongside the pumps. "Here," he added, without waiting for an answer, "get yourselves something. And bring me a bottle of strawberry soda pop, please."

Hildy accepted the silver dollar and thanked him. She and Ruby hurried across the gravel driveway, which smelled of oil. Ben watched the attendant vigorously pump a handle back and forth, causing gasoline to gush into a clear reservoir with gallon markings on it.

Hildy was hungry, but when she entered the dingy cafe, one look made her appetite disappear. Fly season was over, but nobody had bothered to remove the amber-colored fly-paper strips that had been used in the summer. They still hung from the ceiling, covered with flies.

The man at the grill looked up and asked, "What'll you gals have?"

Hildy glanced at the man's unruly brown hair and dirty apron, and said, "I'll take a nickel candy bar and a bottle of soda pop. Take that and whatever my cousin orders out of this." She handed the man the silver dollar, trying not to touch his grimy hand.

Ruby peered through the candy counter glass. "Reckon I'll have me one of them jawbreakers," she said.

Hildy looked a long moment at the variety of wrapped chocolate bars, licking her lips in anticipation. She couldn't remember ever tasting a real chocolate bar. Her mother used to occasionally buy a five-cent bag of candy orange slices for all the girls to share, but there had never been a spare nickel for one child to have a whole candy bar to herself.

Hildy finally made her selection, then went to the icebox. She opened it, took a bottle of strawberry soda, and removed the cap with the opener on the wall.

As she headed for the door, Hildy could see through the

grimy, fly-specked window that Ben was paying the attendant who had pumped the gasoline. At the same time, she noticed a box-shaped, two-door Model T Ford sedan pull up by the water-and-air sign. Steam spouted from the radiator.

Two mattresses were tied on top of the car. The running boards were jammed with cardboard boxes, and bundles swung from the door handles. A lean-faced man sat behind the wheel. A woman, who looked very tired, sat beside him holding a baby in her arms. Two dirty-faced, stringy-haired little girls were perched in the backseat.

The car's occupants turned to look as a California highway patrolman pulled up behind the Model T on a motorcycle, with its red light flashing.

Her curiosity aroused, Hildy opened the door and stepped outside, absently unwrapping the candy bar.

The officer, looking stern in his uniform and military-type puttees, got off his cycle and approached the driver's side. "May I see your driver's license and registration, please?" he asked.

Hildy suspected by the way the driver squirmed that he didn't have a driver's license. She heard him ask the officer, "Why are you stoppin' me?"

"It's against the law to hang objects from the door handles, or let them extend beyond the running board," the patrolman replied. "Now, may I see your license?"

One of the girls in the backseat started to cry. She pleaded, "Don't take my daddy to jail!" She wailed in anguish, and then the other girl started crying.

Hildy couldn't hear the father's reply, but it looked like he was trying in vain to reassure his daughters.

Hildy impulsively walked up to the car. "Excuse me," she said to the officer. "Here, girls." She handed her candy bar to them through the open window. "Don't cry now."

Then she turned and walked away, carrying only the bottle of soda. Aware that the girls had stopped crying, Hildy licked her lips, still wondering what a chocolate bar tasted like.

Ruby came out of the cafe, her right cheek looking somewhat

disfigured from the huge jawbreaker tucked inside. She handed Hildy the change from the dollar and asked, "Why's the policeman givin' that man a ticket?"

Hildy started to explain, then hesitated when she saw a big Cadillac sedan slow down as if to pull off the highway. Hildy got a glimpse of the driver, blinked in surprise, then looked again.

The driver stared at the highway patrolman for a second, then abruptly pulled the Cadillac's front wheels back onto the highway and continued on toward the mountains.

Hildy grabbed Ruby's arm. "Quick!" she whispered urgently, "Get into the car!"

"I'm a-comin'," Ruby mumbled around the jawbreaker. "Ain't no call to go yankin' muh arm off."

Hildy spoke to Brother Ben, "See that big car up ahead? Follow it! It's the same one Ruby and I saw in the barn, and the man driving it is one of the outlaws!"

"You sure about that?" Ben asked, getting into the Packard.

"I'm sure!" Hildy said, sliding into the front seat. "It was Jiggs, the one who wanted to shoot Mischief with a tommy gun. Maybe he'll lead us right to their new hideout—and Dixie Mae."

The old ranger asked, "Was he alone?"

"I think so. Ruby, didn't you see him?"

She removed the jawbreaker from her mouth. "Cain't say's I did, 'cause I was a-watchin' that policeman."

Ben accelerated the Packard on the paved highway and asked, "Do you think he saw you girls?"

"Wouldn't matter," Hildy replied. "He didn't get a look at us in the barn. He only saw Mischief before Dixie Mae's father kicked him out."

"He's never seen me, or this car for that matter," Ben said in his soft drawl. "We should be able to follow him without his getting suspicious. We'll stay behind him a quarter mile or so."

He took the strawberry soda from Hildy and drank it while he drove with the other hand. As the two cars continued into the foothills, a few other vehicles appeared on the road. Some passed the Packard, and the old ranger said that was good because he didn't want to appear to be following the outlaw. He finished his soda and handed the bottle to Hildy. She shoved it under the front seat.

The road became increasingly narrow and full of turns. Periodically, the old ranger sounded his horn going around curves, as the law required. Each time, Hildy held her breath until the Cadillac came into view again.

After about half an hour, the old ranger slowed the car as they approached a small town. As they rounded another curve Hildy blinked in shock.

Only the empty highway stretched ahead.

Hildy sucked in her breath. "He's gone!" She glanced around. Several cars could be seen along the side streets of the small community, but she didn't see the Cadillac.

The old ranger looked around too and said, "He may have gotten suspicious and pulled off to let us pass. But it's more likely that he stopped for gas. He no doubt planned to get gas back there when he saw the highway patrolman. We'll drive on through town and wait out of sight for him to pass."

Hildy was worried about that, but the old ranger drove out of the city limits and parked under a low-spreading live oak just off the highway. The three could see traffic coming up the hill, but the tree hid their car from view.

They sat in anxious silence for several minutes. Hildy wondered, *I'll bet Jiggs was the one who messed up our house. Why else would he be so late starting up to the outlaws' new hideout? Oh, well, it doesn't matter so long as he leads us to Dixie Mae. I just hope we haven't lost him for good.*

"Yonder he comes!" Ruby's sudden exclamation interrupted Hildy's thoughts. She turned to look just as the Cadillac flashed by.

Ben pulled the Packard back onto the highway within seconds, following the cream-colored Cadillac.

Hildy's hopes rose again. "He must have stopped for gas," she said. "Let's hope he goes directly to the hideout and Dixie Mae."

"And let's all pray that he doesn't realize we're following him," Ben replied.

Hildy prayed silently during the next hour, trying not to be anxious as she realized following Jiggs might be the only way to find and rescue Dixie Mae.

"He's slowing down!" Ben exclaimed. "He's turning onto a dirt road."

Hildy saw the big sedan kick up dust. "Do you think it's a trick to see if we'll follow?"

"Hard to tell." Ben eased off on the accelerator and the Packard slowed. "He might be heading for Colfax on that road. I saw a sign back there that pointed in that direction. But there's no other car on the road, so if I follow now, he'll probably get suspicious. I'll pull off the road and watch him awhile."

Hildy didn't like the idea because she was afraid they'd lose their only lead to Dixie Mae, but she also understood the wisdom in holding back.

The old ranger stopped the car on the shoulder and set the handbrake while Hildy and Ruby kept their eyes on the plume of dust thrown up by the outlaw's car. It moved steadily into the distance, appearing smaller and smaller to the girls. Then it vanished around a curve.

"We're going to lose him!" Hildy exclaimed.

"Not if he keeps kicking up all that dust," Ben said, releasing the brake. "We'll be right behind him in a couple of minutes."

Ruby commented, "If'n he looks back, he'll see we'uns are a-kickin' up a big cloud o' dust too."

Hildy felt her insides tighten and her heart speed up, because she realized this was the most critical part of the chase. She tried to relax by thinking of Dixie Mae and how she would react when they found her.

Hildy's thoughts jumped to Spud. *Wish he were here*, she thought with a sigh.

She felt a little strange, thinking about the boy, but in the five months since they'd met, she and Ruby and Spud had gone through many exciting adventures together.

Now Hildy and Ruby faced the prospects of a dangerous situation with nobody but an eighty-six-year-old former U.S. Marshal and Texas Ranger. Hildy had a lot of confidence in Ben Strong, but she wished Spud could share in whatever was about to happen.

"Lookee yonder!" Ruby exclaimed. "Comin' 'round the bend! That thar's one o' them li'l ol' trains!"

"Must be Dead Man's Curve that Mr. Farnham mentioned," Hildy said. "That means Shaw's Summit tunnel is right up there on that mountain. And look, isn't that a schoolhouse off to the—?" The whistle of the approaching train drowned out her words.

The old ranger exclaimed, "The driver of the Cadillac is speeding up! He's going to try to beat the train!"

Hildy held her breath as the outlaw's big vehicle bounced over the crossing seconds before the narrow-gauge locomotive hurtled by with whistle screaming.

Ben pulled the Packard to a stop as the slow-moving train of boxcars, flatcars, and gondolas completely blocked the crossing.

Hildy drummed her fingers impatiently on the dashboard as the train moved ponderously by. "We're going to lose him for sure!"

She glanced anxiously around, but there was nothing to do but wait. Her gaze swept the one-room schoolhouse with the open bell tower over the front door. "Look!" she exclaimed, pointing. "That's it! The sign says TWIN PINES SCHOOL."

"Shore does!" Ruby agreed. "An' here comes the end o' the train!"

With some difficulty, Hildy looked away from the schoolhouse and watched the slow approach of the caboose. When it had passed, she peered anxiously ahead. The road was silent and empty. Even the dust had settled.

Ruby muttered, "He done got clean away!"

Hildy groaned in anguish, "Now, how will we ever find Dixie Mae?"

CHAPTER
THIRTEEN

———

ANOTHER
DISAPPOINTMENT

Thursday Afternoon and Evening

H ildy was keenly disappointed at losing sight of the new
Cadillac driven by Jiggs. She asked, "Brother Ben, how
could he disappear on this deserted country road?"

"He had to have turned off shortly after crossing the tracks,"
the old ranger replied. "I'd guess their new hideout is nearby,
based on the fact that we're close to a couple of landmarks we
know about—the Twin Pines School mentioned in Dixie Mae's
note, and the railroad curve."

Ruby asked, "But whar's the tunnel she tol' us about whar
them outlaws figger to rob the train?"

The old ranger pointed. "I think I know. If you girls follow
the railroad tracks back up around that curve where we first saw
the train, there's a steep grade. See how it goes up that big hill?
My guess is that Shaw's Summit tunnel is at the top of that."

Hildy, Ruby, and Ben sat in silence, sweeping the area with
their gaze. They were high enough in the foothills that oaks,
digger pines, and an occasional ponderosa could be seen scat-

tered over the gently rolling hills stretching up to the mountain ranges.

Ben broke the silence. "There could be a hideout back under those trees or down in the gulches between the hills. If it weren't so late in the day, we could look for tire tracks where the Cadillac left the road, but it'll soon be dark. We'd better get on into town."

Hildy sighed as Brother Ben headed for Quartz City. "I guess it was too good to be true," she mused, "but for a while there, I hoped Jiggs would lead us straight to Dixie Mae."

Ben asked in his soft drawl, "Do you girls know the law of faith?"

Hildy glanced at Ruby, who shrugged, then she turned again to Ben. "I don't think so."

"It's this: 'As thou hast believed, so be it done unto thee.' That's scriptural. Or, as someone said, 'You don't always get what you pray for, but what you expect.' "

Hildy remarked, "I told Dixie Mae that all things are possible to those who believe. She liked that."

To herself, Hildy admitted, *But I'm having doubts myself. But I can't! I've got to keep on believing that we're going to find Dixie Mae, return her to her mother, and stop the gold train robbers. Joey's going to be okay, too. And someday we'll have our "forever" home.*

Ruby asked, "What are ye a-gonna do now, Ben?"

"First," he replied, "I'm going to check into our lodgings. Matt called ahead and made arrangements for all of us to stay at Mrs. Callahan's Room and Board."

Last month Hildy and her father had stayed at the immense, two-story wooden structure only half a block beyond the narrow-gauge railroad tracks. Hildy remembered Mrs. Callahan as a big woman with strong upper arms, a red face, and a voice like a thunderclap.

"Then," Ben continued, "I'll check in with my law-enforcement contacts. I think Skeezix can be trusted, so if you girls don't mind, you could try to find him and see if he can be of any help."

"What about Jack Tremayne?" Ruby asked.

"We'll drive over to his place later," Ben answered. "Since boys often go exploring, I hope he'll know about the places where an outlaw gang might make their hideout around Twin Pines School, even though it's several miles from Quartz City."

Hildy said impulsively, "I wish Spud were here to help!"

Ruby muttered, "I druther have Jack any time than ol' Spud! Him an' his fancy two-dollar words!"

Hildy fought back the impulse to defend Spud. She didn't want to get into an argument with her cousin, so she lapsed into thoughtful silence as the big Packard continued through the foothills toward Quartz City.

It was late in the afternoon when they stopped in front of the boardinghouse. The steady pounding of stamp mills seemed to come from every direction. The stamp mills crushed the hard-rock chunks to release the gold, which had been mined deep underground.

Mrs. Callahan surprised Hildy by throwing her huge arms around her in a big hug. The woman was a little less demon-strative with Ruby and the old ranger, but still gave them a warm welcome.

She asked about Hildy's father while showing the new arri-vals to their accommodations. The girls shared the same adjoin-ing rooms Hildy and her father recently had. The old ranger's room was directly across the hall.

When Mrs. Callahan returned to her quarters, the cousins and the old ranger walked outside. Ben drove toward the police station. The girls buttoned their coats against the November chill.

"Brrr!" Hildy exclaimed. "It's getting colder by the minute. Think it could snow?"

Ruby squinted at the sky. "Wouldn't surprise me none. We'd best find Skeezix, an' git back to our room a-fore we turn to icicles."

The cousins hurried down the steeply inclined street to the two-story depot. They found the retired railroader sitting against the side of the loading platform, whittling. With watery blue eyes, he watched the approaching girls, frowning as though trying to recall who they were.

"Hi!" Hildy called, smiling. "Remember us?"

Skeezix shoved up the bill of his traditional railroader's cap with the blade of his jackknife. He looked frail in striped overalls that were too big for his thin body. His matching coat was frayed, and didn't appear to be warm enough to protect him against the increasing chill of the weather.

"Hildy," he said, returning the smile. "And Ruby, right?" When they nodded, he asked, "What brings you two back to this neck of the woods?"

Hildy quickly told the whole story, including trailing the outlaw Jiggs and losing him near Twin Pines School. She concluded, "So we came to see if you could help us."

"What do you want to know first?" he asked.

"What about the gold train?"

Skeezix pointed to a siding. "Look over there. What do you see?"

Hildy frowned, not understanding. "Just some railroad cars."

"Look again. They're special cars. Every hobo who lives in the jungle around here knows that."

Hildy studied them thoughtfully, then admitted, "They look ordinary to me."

Skeezix lowered his voice. "They're not. Those are part of a gold train."

Hildy questioned, "How do you know that?"

"Shhh!" Skeezix cautioned. Leaning close to both girls he asked in a low voice, "You want to know how I can tell the mines are about to ship some bullion from here to Colfax on this line?"

The girls nodded together, so the railroader explained. "See that wooden car on the end? Looks like it's part passenger coach and part boxcar, doesn't it?"

Hildy nodded. It was the longest of the cars, about sixty feet long. The far end looked exactly like a boxcar with a sliding door. The near end resembled a regular passenger coach with windows and a small observation platform.

Skeezix explained quietly, "They're going to put the gold in the back part of that car. There's a heavy partition between there and the passengers, so of course they won't even know any gold's there, protected by armed guards. Now, what kind of cars do you see next to that?"

Hildy said, "Two flatcars and a tanker." The flatcars were each about thirty-six feet long. The tanker was perhaps five feet longer overall, although the tank itself was about the same length as the flatcar.

Ruby added, "That thar's a boxcar next to them, maybe forty feet long. Lots smaller'n reg'lar train cars. But how kin ye tell that's a-gonna be a gold train?"

" 'Cause the railroad people always make up a gold train the same way. Can you see why?"

Hildy nodded slowly. "The only way to approach the gold car is across two open flatcars. Nobody could sneak up on the guards that way."

"An' the tanker," Ruby added, "is probably full of coal oil er gasoline er somethin', so nobody kin hide in that. But some bandits could hide in them boxcars."

Skeezix shook his head. "No, they can't, because they're always locked and sealed. Once the trucks deliver the gold from the mines to the last car, the locomotive hooks up to all those cars as they're sitting, and off they go to Colfax."

Skeezix paused and looked up, studying the sky. "Depending on the weather, of course. Looks like we're about to get some snow."

"If it snows much, will it stop the train?" Hildy wanted to know.

"Not likely this early in the year. About the only problem with early snow is that it sometimes causes little avalanches that set off rock slides and block the track for a while."

Ruby pulled her jacket tighter about herself and brushed her short blonde hair from her eyes where the wind had blown it. "I'd shore admire to see them load that thar gold. When do ye reckon they'll bring it?"

The railroader shrugged. "Maybe tonight, maybe tomorrow morning. The mine owners like to do that as quietly as possible so that nobody notices. Not that it matters much, because nobody's ever tried to rob the train." He paused, then added, "Until now, I mean."

Ruby asked, "When will that thar ol' train leave?"

"When it's ready. You see, this short line not only doesn't run on a schedule, it's probably the only one in the country that's allowed to run as a mixed train."

"What does that mean?" Hildy asked.

"That means it can carry both passengers and freight cars at the same time—even hazardous materials, like gasoline tankers or dynamite boxcars."

"Dynamite an' gas with passengers?" Ruby gasped. "Yo're a-funnin', ain't ye?"

Skeezix replied, " 'Fraid not. I've seen it myself many times on this line."

Hildy shook her head in disapproval. "I wouldn't want to be a passenger on a train carrying dangerous things like that."

Skeezix chuckled. "The passengers never know about the gold or the hazardous materials."

Hildy asked, "What if there were an accident?"

"Oh, some cars have jumped the track now and then. It's happened a couple of times at Dead Man's Curve. They call it that because a hobo got killed one time when some boxcars rolled over there. You can't run a railroad without some accidents, you know."

Hildy was glad she and her friends had no plans to ride the train. She stood up and started to thank Skeezix for his help, then thought of something else.

"You know anything about Shaw's Summit tunnel or Twin Pines School?"

"I used to pass the school when I was still working on the

railroad. As for the tunnel—that's a flat area with nothing but two railroad spurs and a depot. Lonesome kind of place where cars are sometimes taken off the siding and put into the train, or the other way 'round. Pretty routine."

He paused, then added, "Except for the time the train crew left a flatcar of lumber on the main line without setting the brake."

"What happened?" Hildy wanted to know.

"That's the start of the steep grade to Dead Man's Curve, so the car started rolling downhill. The brakeman saw it and ran after it, but he couldn't get aboard. Ordinarily, this narrow gauge doesn't go much faster than twenty miles an hour behind a locomotive. But that lone runaway car reached about sixty miles an hour going downhill. Jumped the track at Dead Man's Curve, of course. Threw that lumber everywhere."

Hildy remembered the proximity of the Twin Pines School to the curve. She asked, "Anybody get hurt?"

"Not a soul. Naturally, nobody was on the car, and it was Saturday, so there were no kids at the school. Good thing, too. Some of those pieces of lumber were thrown so hard, they punched holes in the side of the school nearest the tracks. 'Course, the train crew got fired for leaving a car unattended on the main line."

The cousins thanked Skeezix for his help and walked back to the boardinghouse. They arrived just as the old ranger drove up. He motioned for them to get in. When they were seated, he eased the car away from the high curb.

Hildy asked, "What did you find out from your law-enforcement people?"

"Not much, I'm afraid. There's nothing new from the informant. I just filled everyone in on what we know and headed back here."

"We a-headin' fer Jack's house now?" Ruby asked.

"Yup! Going to see if he can give us any help on this case. What did you girls learn from Skeezix?"

The cousins reported what he'd told them, focusing on the

fact that the gold train was ready to roll, except for having the gold trucked over from the mines, and the locomotive and tender hooked up.

"So," Hildy concluded, "it looks like we have only a few hours to stop the robbery and find Dixie Mae."

"Let's hope Jack can help," the old ranger said. "I think I remember how to get to his place."

With Hildy's help, Ben drove directly to the small frame house on the outskirts of Quartz Hill. He left the headlights on because there were no streetlights. Ruby volunteered to go to the door, and Hildy watched her walk up the dirt path and onto the small front porch.

"Sure hope he's home," Hildy said to Ben as Ruby knocked.

The porch light came on, and a middle-aged man opened the door.

Hildy exclaimed, "That's not Jack, and his father's dead! Wonder who it is?" She frowned as the man shook his head, and Ruby turned and left the porch. Hildy opened the car door for her.

Ruby announced, "Guess what? Jack an' his whole family moved a coupla weeks ago. Y'all will never guess whar they live."

"Ruby," Hildy exclaimed, "don't stall! Tell us!"

Ruby's grin showed in the pale light of the dashboard. "Out in the country by Twin Pines School! I got directions. Ye wanna go thar now?"

Hildy looked expectantly at the old ranger. He nodded. "I know you must be hungry, because I am. But time's running out. We'd better go find Jack first."

Half an hour later, following Ruby's directions, they found the house where Jack Tremayne lived. But it was dark, and nobody answered Ruby's knock.

Hildy looked at the old ranger. "Another disappointment! What can we do now?"

Chapter Fourteen

SURPRISE VISITORS

Thursday Night

B en looked thoughtful. "We don't have any idea where Jack or his family might be, or where to look for them. Even the neighbors' houses are dark, so we can't ask them. We may as well go get some supper."

Hildy asked, "Could you drive by Twin Pines School? I'd like to take a better look at it."

Ben agreed, and soon they approached the one-room school. There were many cars parked along the dirt shoulder, and electric lights were on at the school.

Ruby remarked, "Maybe they's havin' a Thanksgiving program. Could we'uns stop an' see if'n Jack's thar?"

The old ranger nodded and parked behind the last car. Buttoning their coats against the increasingly sharp night wind, Hildy, Ruby, and Ben walked down the gravel road past the parked cars.

They found their way by the light of two large outside electric lights. One was on top of a wooden pole in front of the white, single-story frame school building. This lighted the entrance to the school and the wooden flagpole nearby. A second outdoor light was positioned just under the roof of an adjacent two-story tank house to illuminate the yard between the two buildings.

A couple of bicycles lay beside the concrete steps at the front of the school. Hildy hoped to recognize the one she'd seen Dixie Mae riding near Lone River, but these were boys' bikes.

Hildy, Ruby, and Ben entered the short hallway, lined with hanging coats and hats. Shelves had been built above to hold lunch buckets. These were empty except for a few books and an umbrella. Young voices could be heard through the doors leading to the classroom.

Hildy peeked in and saw several children dressed in Pilgrim costumes, putting on a play in the space between the blackboard and the desks. Other students and some parents sat at the desks. A few men leaned against the back and side walls of the room.

"Thar's Jack!" Ruby whispered. He was also dressed as a Pilgrim.

Jack Tremayne, son of a deceased Cornish deep-rock miner, was a slender boy, taller than Hildy or Ruby. He had straight dark hair and a strong chin. Hildy knew that Ruby, at least, thought Jack was good-looking.

She and Ruby had met the blue-eyed boy last month when he was looking for bits of gold-bearing ore in a dump outside a deep-rock mine. The cousins had helped Jack solve a mystery about how his father was killed. But that was past, and Hildy wished the play were over, too, because tomorrow the bandits were supposed to rob the gold train. If they succeeded, the chances of finding and rescuing Dixie Mae were almost nonexistent.

After a hurried consultation, Hildy, Ruby, and Ben quietly slipped inside the classroom, where it was warmer, and they could watch the conclusion of the school play.

When it was over, Hildy led the way among students and parents to where Jack stood.

"Hi," Hildy said, smiling at him. "Remember us?"

"Of course!" Jack exclaimed, returning the smile. "Hildy and Ruby—and Ben Strong. What brings you here?"

Hildy glanced around and lowered her voice. "Could we talk privately? It's pretty important."

"Sure! Wait'll I change into my regular clothes. We can talk outside."

The wind had picked up by the time they all stepped out into the night. Jack was appropriately dressed in high-topped boots, blue jeans, and a heavy, blue corduroy jacket with a sheepskin collar.

Jack explained that his mother had found a job taking care of an old woman who lived nearby in exchange for room and board for the Tremayne family.

Hildy, Ruby, and Ben briefly told Jack why they were here, and that they needed his help.

"After what you did for me last month," the boy said seriously, "I'll do anything. What do you want me to do?"

Hildy asked, "Did a girl named Dixie Mae attend school here today?"

"No, there've been no new students in the school since our family moved here."

"Where's the most logical place a gang would hide out near here?" Hildy wanted to know.

"Oh, let's see. I know of three or four abandoned houses back in the trees."

"Where's Shaw's Summit tunnel?" Ben asked.

"Follow the road that runs by the school to the top of that steep grade. Can't miss it."

Ruby asked, "Have ye seen any strangers a-drivin' trucks er a new Cadillac sedan 'round here?"

"I don't remember any trucks, but on our way over here tonight, I noticed a brand-new, light-colored Cad just pulling into the parking lot at the bar." He pointed. "It's over in that direction."

Hildy exclaimed, "Of course! It makes sense to me now. Ruby and I saw Jiggs drinking out of a jug he'd hidden in the barn."

Ben said, "This may be the break we've been looking for.

Jack, introduce us to your mother. Maybe she'll let you show us where that place is."

A few minutes later, the four of them approached a small wooden building with a garish sign: FRED'S ROADHOUSE. Jack explained that the bar had been a speakeasy during Prohibition.

Hildy knew that Prohibition began in 1919 when the Eighteenth Amendment to the Constitution had been enacted, and that Prohibition was repealed last year by the Twenty-first Amendment. In between amendments, "the noble experiment," as it was sometimes called, made it illegal to sell liquor in America. However, many people managed to get around the law with "bathtub gin" and other hard liquor sold through roadhouses or speakeasies.

Jack recalled, "My father sometimes made a home brew, but the bottles always blew up."

"That was fairly common when people made their own beer," Ben said as he pulled off the road. He disregarded the small parking lot and parked on the shoulder just beyond the bar. Hildy got out with the others. A blast of cold air made her shiver. She tucked her chin into her jacket collar. "Let's hurry before we freeze," she urged.

The plaintive lyrics to a popular mountain ballad, "May I Sleep in Your Barn Tonight, Mister?" could be heard through the walls of the frame structure. Hildy knew that the sad lyrics depicted a tramp in the rain. Songs about tramps were popular because, as the Depression continued, the country was full of such people.

Hildy joined the others in looking for Jiggs' Cadillac. Lights hanging from overhead wires bounced in the wind and illuminated the parking lot. There was no immediate sign of the deluxe sedan, and Ben suggested they spread out through the lot.

Ben and Jack started at the far end while Hildy and Ruby searched the row of cars nearest the building. There were no other people in sight. The band inside swung into another tramp tune, "The Big Rock Candy Mountain." The song made Hildy think of Spud, who had once been a hobo.

Hildy was disappointed after their vain search. She and Ruby went to find the old ranger and Jack as the band struck up another favorite, "The Strawberry Roan." Hildy knew her cowboy father liked the song about the horse that couldn't be "rode," and she wondered how he and Molly and the kids were doing.

"Nothing here," Ben said as the four headed for the Packard. "We better take Jack home and get back to Quartz City."

They made arrangements to pick up Jack about seven o'clock the next morning. That would give him more than an hour before school started in which to point out the location of abandoned houses where the outlaws might be hiding out with Dixie Mae.

It was too late to get supper at the boardinghouse, so Ben, Hildy, and Ruby stopped at a small cafe at the edge of Quartz City. They took a booth in the back corner.

Ruby grumbled, "They ain't much chance left fer us to do any o' them things we talked about doin' on the drive up here. Time's practic'ly run out."

Hildy reflected on that as she asked to be excused to wash her hands. The man who served as cook and waiter told her the washroom was around in back, outside. Hildy grabbed her coat and hurried out the door.

Ruby's right, Hildy admitted to herself, hesitating at the entrance to the alley. She was reluctant to step into the dark, unpaved area, but it was quiet, and she could see her way by a distant streetlight. She hurried past some Chinese trees of heaven and found the door to the washroom.

There's so little time left to find Dixie Mae and stop the gold train from being robbed tomorrow, Hildy told herself as she twisted the electric light switch inside. *It just doesn't seem possible.*

Hildy struggled with these thoughts while she dried her hands. When she pushed the door open, it swung out, almost hitting a man.

"Hey, watch it!" he grumbled, his face muted in the shadows. He ducked his head down and walked off.

Hildy started to mumble an apology, then stopped. Her heart

sped up as she recognized Jiggs' voice.

She debated what to do. *If I run inside to tell Ruby and Brother Ben, I'll lose him. And though it would be dangerous to follow him, he might lead me to Dixie Mae.*

Hildy impulsively trailed the outlaw down the alley. The spindly trunks and slender barren limbs of the Chinese trees of heaven rattled ominously. The light at the far end of the alley made the bandit's shadow fall behind him, blending with the deeper shadows of the night. Hildy's heart thudded faster and faster.

Suddenly Jiggs whirled around. "Hey! You following me?" he growled.

Hildy stopped uncertainly. "I—I was just returning to the restaurant."

"You sound like a gal."

Hildy tried to decide whether or not to run the other way. "Y—yes."

"Come closer so I can get a look at you."

"I—I've really got to get back inside. My friends—" The words stuck in her throat as Jiggs stalked toward her.

Hildy turned and fled down the alley, her braids flying in the wind. Trying to keep from stumbling, she ran until she couldn't hear Jiggs behind her. She slowed and looked back. She caught a brief glimpse of the man's face under the distant street-lamp as he turned the corner and into the street.

Breathing hard, Hildy momentarily argued with herself about what to do. Then, cautiously, she tiptoed toward the streetlight. Holding her breath, she peered around the corner of an adobe brick building with rusty iron shutters. The big Cadillac pulled away from the high curb and sped past her.

Hildy watched the taillights until they vanished into the night, heading out of town. Then she rushed into the cafe and told the others what she'd seen.

The old ranger shook his head. "There's no way we could find and follow him now. We might as well eat."

Hildy sighed in frustration and picked up the menu.

Ruby was facing the front door, and looked up. "Lookee yonder!" she exclaimed. "Through the front winder. Ain't that Mr. Farnham's car a-stoppin' outside?"

Hildy and the old ranger looked. They could see by the streetlight that the Pierce Arrow was pulling up directly behind the Packard.

Ben mused, "Wonder what he's doing here?"

Hildy had an anxious feeling as the banker slid out from behind the wheel. *Hope he's not bringing bad news about Joey!* she thought. Hildy followed Ben and Ruby out of the booth. She glanced out the window just as the door on the passenger side of the car opened.

"It's Spud!" she exclaimed.

Ruby muttered under her breath, "Reckon we'uns have troubles a-plenty without him!"

Hildy was so glad to see her friend that she didn't caution Ruby this time to watch her tongue.

After greetings were exchanged, the dapper little banker explained, "Spud and I got to talking, and decided that time is short and you could probably use some extra help. He and I were on our way to Mrs. Callahan's Room and Board when we spotted your car. Any news?"

"Yes," Hildy said as they entered the cafe. She quickly related all that had happened since they left Lone River, including her recent encounter with Jiggs in the alley.

Back at the booth, Mr. Farnham and Spud took off their coats, pulled up extra chairs, and sat down. Hildy sat across from Spud, with Ruby beside her.

Ruby leaned close and whispered in Hildy's ear, "Whatcha grinnin' at ol' Spud like that fer?"

Hildy blinked, unaware her happiness at seeing Spud showed. She decided not to answer her cousin, but turned instead to the banker and asked what he and Spud had been doing since they last met.

"Nothing much," Mr. Farnham said. "It seems all the action is up here."

During the meal, the five discussed plans for the next day. The men agreed to meet at six o'clock in the morning at the boardinghouse. They would drive out with the young people to meet Jack.

That settled, they walked outside. Hildy was surprised that the wind had died down, but it was colder than before. She said good-night to Spud and Mr. Farnham, then Ben drove the girls back to their lodgings.

In her room Hildy pulled off her coat and sat down on the single bed. She said, "It sure feels good to know Spud's going to help us tomorrow."

Ruby wrinkled her nose. "Havin' more people ain't a-gonna he'p us none, 'specially him," she groused. "Time's a runnin' out, an' that's somethin' a whole passel o' people cain't change."

Hildy cautioned, "Remember what Brother Ben said about the law of faith."

"Time a-runnin' out is the same as a law, only—" She stopped abruptly as a knock came at the door.

"I'll get it," Hildy said. "Must be Brother Ben." She opened the door and gasped in surprise. "Skeezix!"

The old man brushed light snow off his coat and looked around the room. "You two alone?" he asked in a low voice.

"Yes. Brother Ben's across the hall," Hildy said. "Do you want to see him?"

Skeezix nodded. "Sure do! And fast! I got some news all of you will want to know right now!"

CHAPTER
FIFTEEN

—

TRACKS IN THE SNOW

Thursday Night and Early Friday Morning

W hen Hildy knocked, the old ranger opened his door. Hildy barely noticed that he was bareheaded and in his stockingfeet as she explained, "Skeezix is here with some news that he says we should hear right away."

"Come in," Ben said, throwing the door open. "Excuse my appearance, I was just getting ready for bed. Skeezix, you take the chair. You girls can sit on the bed, and I'll turn up my suitcase and sit on the end of it."

Hildy glanced around to see that the room was very much like her own. There was an ancient dresser with a corner broken off the mirror. An enamelware washpan and pitcher stood on a small, rickety table. The chair Skeezix sat on was an old straight-backed one that stood beside the small potbelly stove. The single bed completed the meager furnishings.

Through the grimy windowpane, Hildy could see that a light snow was falling.

"Skeezix, what's yore news?" Ruby blurted out.

The retired railroader wiped melted snow from his face before answering. "I overheard a couple of 'boes talking when I walked past the jungle a while ago. I thought maybe—what's the matter, Ruby?"

" 'Boes? Jungle? What do ye mean?" she asked.

Skeezix smiled. " 'Bo is short for hobo. You know—a tramp. The places where they live are called hobo jungles. They're made of old cardboard, wood, tin, anything they can find."

Ruby said, "I knowed that. I jist fergot."

"Go on, Skeezix," Hildy urged. "What did they say?"

"Well, one was tellin' the other that he rode in on the last train coming from Colfax. Got on at Shaw's Summit."

As he paused, Hildy leaned forward. "And?" she prompted, sensing something exciting was about to be told.

"The hobo who was doing the talking said he had been sleeping in an abandoned house not far from Dead Man's Curve when some men came in and ran him off."

"When?" the old ranger asked sharply.

"Yesterday. They came in trucks."

"And a Cadillac?" Ruby asked.

Skeezix shook his head. "No car, just trucks."

Ben looked at the girls. "That explains why we saw the man you call Jiggs on the road coming up from the valley. He apparently stayed behind to vandalize your house, Hildy. The leader must have ridden up with the other outlaws in the trucks."

Hildy asked breathlessly, "Did the tramp say anything about seeing a girl?"

"Sure did! The 'bo mentioned that she was about twelve, and had red hair."

"Dixie Mae!" Hildy exclaimed.

Ben asked, "Skeezix, did this hobo say how many men he'd seen? Or how many trucks?"

"Can't say as he did."

Ruby said, "Me an' Hildy seen three trucks parked in that ol' barn. So if'n they all came up here, that's at least three drivers, not counting Jiggs in the Cadillac."

Hildy added, "And maybe Dixie Mae's father—I mean, if he didn't drive. So that's at least five men."

The old ranger frowned thoughtfully. "It'd take more than that to carry the gold bullion from the train, because each ingot weighs eighty-nine pounds. There are probably eight to ten men, minimum. That's a lot to try capturing at once."

Hildy was sure that was true, but she wanted more information from Skeezix. She asked, "Did that hobo say exactly where this house was that the outlaws took over?"

"No, but he mentioned there was a tree in the yard with the top burned off. Probably hit by lightning. I remember seeing a tree like that when I rode—"

"Can you take us there?" Ben interrupted.

"In daylight, sure. Don't know if I could find it in this snow, especially if it gets heavier."

"Can you be here at six o'clock tomorrow morning?" Ben asked.

"I'll be here," Skeezix said as he stood.

———

Hildy awakened to the sound of heavy boots clumping down the hallway outside her door. *Must be the miners going to work,* she thought. Then her mind leaped to the dramatic realization: *Today's the day!*

She sat up in bed, shaking her long, loose hair from her eyes. She glanced out the window. It was still dark outside, but there was a strange brightness. Everything was covered with a magnificent blanket of fresh snow. Even the narrow-gauge locomotive on the tracks wore a white mantle.

Hildy wasn't sure what time it was, but she guessed that miners leaving the boardinghouse for work meant it was time for her to get up. She pulled a blanket off the bed, threw it over her shoulders against the room's chill, and padded barefoot into the next room to wake Ruby.

Hildy briefly considered lighting the wood-burning stove, but decided against it. The blanket still around her shoulders, she stopped at the washstand. She poured water from the pitcher into the basin and vigorously scrubbed her face. The water seemed just short of freezing, forcing Hildy to finish in seconds.

She dried her face, tossed the blanket back on the bed, and dressed quickly, shivering in the unheated room.

Lord, she prayed silently, *help us to find and rescue Dixie Mae today, and stop the bandits from robbing the train. They all belong in jail.*

She had just finished braiding her hair with the aid of her cracked dresser mirror when there was a knock on the door. Hildy went to answer it, calling, "Ruby, Brother Ben's here."

"I'm a'ready a-goin' a mile a minute," Ruby grumbled.

Hildy opened the hallway door and smiled in surprise at Ben, Spud, Mr. Farnham, and Skeezix.

Spud pushed his aviator goggles up from his forehead, causing a wisp of auburn hair to fall down over his green eyes. He asked, "Ready to undertake unforeseen danger involving risks from vicious adversaries in order to extricate Dixie Mae from her abductors?"

Before Hildy could answer, Ruby came up behind her, muttering, "I'd shore admire to git Dixie Mae an' leave ol' Spud behind with them outlaws."

Hildy spoke quickly, hoping Spud hadn't heard Ruby. "I can hardly wait! I'll get my coat, then we can go pick up Jack."

"First," the old ranger said, "we'll have breakfast and talk over our strategy."

The banker added, "We've also got to talk about a small new complication."

"That's right," Spud agreed, holding up his gloved hands to show they were already wet and dirty. "Ben, I hope you have chains for the Packard. Uncle Matt has some, but they don't fit right. We had to walk over."

"I've got chains," Ben assured the boy. "But we can't comfortably fit seven people in my car."

"Six," Hildy said, glancing around. "You, Mr. Farnham, Spud, Skeezix, Ruby, and me."

"Yo're fergittin' Jack," Ruby muttered. "I guess somebody'll have to stay behind—like you, Spud."

Hildy protested, "We can't do that!"

Ben opened the outside door, letting in a gust of frigid air, "Let's talk about it over breakfast."

It had stopped snowing, but dawn was still about half an hour away when they entered the same little cafe where they'd met the night before. A serious discussion led by Ben and Mr. Farnham finally resulted in a decision. The banker summarized: "Then we're agreed that Ben will drive, taking both girls, because they alone can identify two of the outlaws and Dixie Mae. Skeezix, you'll need to show Ben where to locate that lightning-blasted tree. Jack will need to ride along to show you around the area, including Shaw's Summit tunnel."

Hildy asked, "What about Spud and you, Mr. Farnham?"

"I'll stay here and see if I can find some chains that will fit. If I do, I'll drive up and meet you at Shaw's Summit. Of course, it could clear and the sun come out and melt the snow in a couple of hours. Chains wouldn't be necessary, then. Spud, I guess that means you'd better stay with me."

Hildy felt keenly disappointed and glanced at her cousin. Ruby started to smile, apparently satisfied that Spud wasn't going along. Then Ruby's smile faded as she returned Hildy's gaze.

Ruby cleared her throat. "Lookee here. Y'all are fergittin' somethin'."

"What's that?" the banker asked.

"Jack's only goin' to ride along fer a spell, then he's got to git back to school," Ruby observed. "Spud could go along after all. Reckon we'uns could squeeze him in till Jack's through."

Hildy smiled her appreciation. Ruby's suggestion was an obvious sacrifice on her part.

The old ranger and the banker looked at each other and shrugged. Mr. Farnham said, "Finish your breakfast then, and you can be on your way."

The chains made for a slower trip, and the group in the Packard arrived at Jack's house a little past daylight, about seven o'clock. The miner's son greeted everyone, smiling broadly at Ruby, who sat in the backseat with Hildy and Spud. Jack slid into the front seat, and was introduced to Skeezix. Ben turned the Packard toward Twin Pines School, explaining to Jack why Skeezix was with them.

"The house with the blasted tree in front of it was one of those I was going to show you," Jack said.

"Then we'll go there first," Ben decided. "But remember, we're just going to scout around to see if there's any sign of the outlaws. If there is, I'll go phone my law-enforcement contacts and let them handle it."

"What about Dixie Mae?" Hildy asked anxiously.

The old ranger shrugged. "We'll do whatever we can to rescue her, of course. But we can't even discuss how to do that until we know more than we do now."

Hildy knew that was true, but it still made her anxious. She tried to relax a little, but was too excited as Twin Pines School came into view. Then they passed it, and the Packard approached the railroad tracks at Dead Man's Curve.

"That's whar we done lost that ol' Jiggs yesti'dy," Ruby reminded them.

Hildy nodded, leaning forward to peer out between Skeezix and the old ranger as the big car began to slip and slide. There were no other tire tracks, telling them that theirs was the first vehicle to drive along the remote, rural road that morning.

Suddenly Hildy tensed, straining to see ahead. "Look!" she exclaimed, pointing at the road. "Tire tracks! They come out of that side road to the right and lead up toward the mountain!"

Jack said, "Straight ahead is the way to Shaw's Summit tunnel. Those tracks come from the side road that leads to the old house with the blasted tree."

Ben slowed the Packard, and the chains made less of a clanking sound. "Looks to me like we're too late. Our birds have flown the coop. But we'll stop to make sure."

Moments later, shivering from the cold, Hildy stood with the others as the old ranger finished his inspection.

"The tracks are from three trucks and a car," he announced. "All with chains. The tracks are fresh, made since it stopped snowing. Those men aren't far ahead of us."

"Where's Dixie Mae?" Hildy asked anxiously.

"We'll drive in and take a look at the old house," Ben answered, "to make sure she's not there. But my guess is that they took her along. They're surely planning for everyone to take off for parts unknown after they rob the train."

"But," Skeezix reminded them, "nobody knows just when that train's going to run, so the gang has to be holed up somewhere, waiting near the point where they intend to attack."

"You mean, we've still got time to find them and rescue Dixie Mae?" Hildy asked.

"Looks like it," the old ranger replied, leading the way back to the car. "Those tracks should be easy to follow. Come on, everybody, we may finally be getting a break in this case."

Hildy's heart pounded as the Packard climbed the grade. It was light enough now, and Ben turned off the headlights. Although the sky was still overcast, it was plain to see where the outlaws' tires had flattened the snow, making it possible for Ben to drive a little faster. Hildy noticed that everyone in the car was leaning forward, carefully scanning the tire tracks to make sure they didn't turn off into one of the occasional side roads.

The car topped the steep incline where the road leveled out for a few yards and started down again.

Suddenly, Hildy pointed to the bottom of the hill. "Look! Several cars, but no trucks."

Jack explained the reason for the traffic. "That's the intersection of the most direct county road running between Quartz City and Colfax. Shaw's Summit is just ahead of us on this road."

Ben said in his soft drawl, "If those outlaws turned off on that crossroad, their tracks will blend with all the others that have traveled there this morning, and we won't be able to follow them. We won't even know which direction they went."

As the Packard slowed for the intersection, Hildy could tell that no vehicle had gone up the grade toward Shaw's Summit.

Ruby whispered, "They ain't hardly no time left to find Dixie Mae er stop the train robbery, an' we done lost them crooks with no way to find 'em—none a-tall!"

—

Chapter Sixteen

DANGER ON THE RAILS

Friday Morning

As the old ranger drove on toward Shaw's Summit, Hildy tried hard to not be discouraged. She reminded herself of what she had told Dixie Mae: *All things are possible to him who believes.* But doubts continued to attack Hildy's mind, tearing away at her faith.

Spud sat next to Hildy in the backseat and roused her from her brooding. "Why the introspection?" he asked in a low voice.

Hildy smiled in spite of herself, glancing at Ruby to see if she'd noticed Spud's use of what she called a "two-dollar word." But Ruby was leaning forward, talking to Jack in the front seat.

Hildy was usually reluctant to reveal her innermost thoughts, but she felt comfortable sharing her doubts with Spud. She did so in low tones so nobody else could hear.

When she finished, Spud's green eyes focused on her with a softness she'd never seen before.

He said, "I was starting to feel doubts myself. But it's not fair that both of us doubt at the same time. Let's take turns. You want to go first, or should I?"

Hildy studied him thoughtfully, barely detecting a hint of his

129

teasing smile. Suddenly she laughed aloud. "You're trying to kid me out of feeling this way!"

He grinned broadly and lightly touched the back of her hand. "Did it work?" he asked.

Hildy nodded, feeling a strange warmth surge through her. "Yes," she replied softly, "it worked."

"Good!" Spud removed his hand, suddenly aware that it had touched hers. "Let's enjoy the scenery, because we may be very busy soon, and won't have time to enjoy it."

The sky was clearing as the Packard climbed steadily up the side of a steep mountain through stately ponderosa pines, low-growing live oaks, and deciduous black oaks. All were lightly covered with new-fallen snow.

Hildy's thoughts jumped to her little brother. *Wonder how Joey's doing?* She tried to tell herself that he would be fine. But she still felt concern as Jack spoke from the front seat, announcing that Shaw's Summit was just around the next curve.

Hildy leaned forward, knowing this was the spot Dixie Mae had indicated her father and his gang planned to attack the gold train.

The old ranger said, "I doubt the outlaws will be foolish enough to show themselves before they see or hear the train coming, but we can't be too careful. Hildy and Ruby, you're the only ones who have seen Dixie Mae. You'd both better keep a sharp eye out for her. The rest of us can look for that Cadillac and the three trucks."

Hildy's eager eyes took in the scene as the Packard rounded the curve. Shaw's Summit was little more than a wide, flat place beside a country road. The few acres between two small mountain ranges glistened in full sunshine. Hildy squinted against the sudden glare.

To the west, the way the Packard had come, Hildy saw a small frame house with a corrugated tin roof, almost hidden behind old cedars. To the north, the main-line tracks emerged from a hundred-foot long tunnel cut from solid rock. Across the tracks to the east, Hildy saw two spurs with a few rail cars.

Beyond them, a tiny wooden depot stood in desolate silence. To the south, at the end of the flat area past the unpaved road, the main line seemed to drop rather sharply.

Skeezix explained, "That's the start of the downhill grade to Dead Man's Curve by Twin Pines School. From there the tracks go into Colfax."

"I don't see or hear anything," Spud announced. "Looks like a perfect setting to ambush a train."

Ben said, "I'll pull around that next curve out of sight. Then we can all walk back and take a quick look around. We need to see the lay of the land before we take Jack back to school."

"I'll miss all the excitement," Jack protested.

"We sure don't want to spook Stonecipher before we're sure of their position and law-enforcement officers can arrive to deal with them," Ben answered. "I'd like everybody safely away from here before the robbery begins."

"What about Mr. Farnham?" Hildy asked. "He said he'd meet us here if he could get some tire chains."

"He won't stop if we're not here," Ben assured her. "And he certainly wouldn't stop if he saw the robbery was in progress. Let's hurry our inspection."

Ben parked the car in some dense manzanita off the road and led the way along the short walk back to the flat. Hildy realized that she hadn't seen or heard another car since crossing the main county-road intersection. She decided that Shaw's Summit was a lonely place. Yet there was a certain beauty about the solitude.

A mountain rose sharply to a peak about two hundred feet above the tunnel. The steep sides were covered with pines, oaks, manzanita, and other native brush.

Ben spoke up. "Those bandits could arrive any minute. Spread out and notice everything. We'll compare notes when we get back to the car."

Hildy asked, "Are we looking for anything in particular?"

"Yup!" Ben replied. "The gang has to stop the train, and we have to try to figure out how they plan to do that. There's no water tank, so the engine won't stop for water. There are no passengers around; in fact, nobody's at the depot, so the train won't stop there either. However, because gold is very heavy, Stonecipher's men have to attack the train near this road. Those trucks would get stuck in the snow or mud if they drove off the road."

Hildy looked toward the roof of the little house she'd glimpsed behind some cedar trees. Skeezix explained that train crews sometimes stayed there.

Hildy asked, "Do you suppose Dixie Mae could be held prisoner in that house?"

"It's not likely," Skeezix answered. "Bandits would be foolish to risk doing that. Because none of the trains on this short line run on a schedule, a train crew could show up at the house at any time."

"Just the same, I think I'll check it out," Hildy announced. She started forward, then pointed to the spur nearest the main line. A strange contraption rested on the narrow-gauge rails. "What's that, Skeezix?"

"A gasoline-powered switcher," he replied. "It's a small engine used to shunt cars like those over there. The switcher can move them from the main line to the spurs, or the other way around."

Hildy looked at the cars the old railroader had indicated. There was a gasoline tank car, three boxcars, and an old wooden passenger coach on the second spur. The snow on the equipment had already started to melt.

Hildy thanked Skeezix and again turned toward the small house. When Spud fell into step beside her, she felt good. Ruby and Jack headed toward the tunnel while Ben and Skeezix walked between the tiny depot, the switcher, and the silent cars on the sidings.

The air was brisk, but the sun was bright, making everyone squint at its reflection off the snow. Hildy still felt anxious, knowing that the robbers could arrive at any minute; and even if Dixie Mae were with them, Hildy realized she hadn't the faintest idea of how to rescue the red-haired girl.

Suddenly Hildy tensed, stopping still on the gravel beside the main line. She whispered, "Spud, there's somebody over there by the house!"

Before the boy could reply, Hildy heard Ruby let out a happy shout. "Look out, Jack!" Ruby warned, "I'm a-gonna hit ye with a snowball!"

Hildy stared into the cedars where she'd seen somebody move. She heard Jack yell back at Ruby.

"You do and I'll turn you into a snowman!"

Hildy had never thought she'd see the day when her tomboy cousin would show an interest in boys, but now Hildy's focus was on the figure she'd glimpsed beyond the cedars.

"There!" she whispered to Spud. "See him?"

Before Spud could reply, a short man in a heavy coat, railroader's cap, and gloves stepped from behind the trees near the house. He called in a firm, but not a loud voice, "Hey, you kids, don't yell!"

Hildy was relieved that the stranger seemed to be a railroad man. Then she turned to see that not only were Ruby and Jack staring at the man, but so were Ben and Skeezix.

Ben started walking toward him. "What's the problem, mister? They're not doing any harm."

"Not yet," the short man answered, "but they could." He gestured toward the mountain towering behind them. "We had a rock slide the other side of the tunnel a while ago. If somebody makes just the right noise, all that snow on the hillside could come shooting down, causing an avalanche that could close both ends of the tunnel, maybe even hurt somebody."

"I'm plumb sorry, mister," Ruby apologized. "Me an' Jack didn't mean no harm."

"It's okay," the short man answered. "I've put in a call on the company's private line for them to send the powder monkey to blast that snow loose. He can place his charges in such a way that the snow and rocks fall clear of the tunnel. But he can't get here until this afternoon, so you'll have to keep the noise down."

"We'll do that," Ben said. "We're going to be here only a few minutes anyway."

Hildy turned to Spud. "Is that true? Can noise really cause an avalanche?"

"So I've heard."

The old ranger said, "I'm sorry to cut your fun short, but maybe we'd better just skip looking around anymore and get Jack back to school."

"What about Mr. Farnham?" Hildy asked. "What if he comes while we're away?"

"He'll wait for us," the old ranger replied.

Spud said, "It won't take you long to drop Jack off and return. I'll wait here for Uncle Matt."

Skeezix offered, "I'll stay with you, Spud."

Hildy added, "I'll stay, too."

"Reckon I'll ride along with Jack an' Ben," Ruby said casually.

Ben shook his head. "Your fathers said you two girls have to stay together. Remember?"

Ruby made a strangled sound in her throat that told Hildy how much her cousin wanted to be with Jack as long as she could.

Hildy said, "You're right. I'll ride down to the school, too."

Ruby hesitated, looking at Jack. "Reckon I'd best stay with Hildy after all. She might need me in case Dixie Mae an' them outlaws show up. Ye un'erstand, don't ye Jack?"

He smiled. "I do. Duty first."

The old ranger frowned. "Well, I guess it's all right, since none of the outlaws have ever seen any of you. Even if they're watching, they'd have no reason to be suspicious. But be careful, anyway."

Jack gave Ruby a tender smile, then walked with Ben to the Packard.

When the car had turned around and headed west around the curve, Ruby suggested she and Hildy explore the tunnel.

Skeezix said, "I don't see any harm in that. You kids go ahead, but stay close by. I'll go over and talk to that railroader."

Ruby hurried ahead of Hildy and Spud, leaving them to walk on the railroad ties leading to the tunnel.

Hildy commented, "It's sure quiet up here. There hasn't been another car or another human being except that man who asked us not to make noise."

"That's why the brigands chose this remote site to achieve their nefarious objective," Spud spoke knowingly.

"But how are they going to stop the train?" Hildy asked.

"They've got to block the tracks somehow. But I don't see any boulders, logs, or anything that could be used for that purpose."

Hildy could see her cousin's silhouette at the far end of the tunnel as she and Spud entered the south end. The walls were solid rock. Smoke from the oil-burning locomotives had blackened the ceiling. Between the walls and the tracks, on both sides, there was a graveled space of about three feet.

Hildy sighed. "I sure wish we could find Dixie Mae. I doubt we'll have much chance once the robbery takes place."

As Hildy and Spud exited the tunnel, Hildy stopped in surprise. Ruby had walked out onto the railroad trestle, which stretched a quarter mile across a dry riverbed a hundred feet below.

Hildy raised her voice in alarm, "Come back before you fall!"

Ruby called over her shoulder, "I ain't skeered." She kept walking, arms outstretched, balancing herself while stepping from one crosstie to another.

"She's just showing off," Spud said. "Let's wait here for her to come to her senses and return."

"I can't! I've got to stay with her!"

Very reluctantly, Hildy started across the trestle, carefully placing her feet on the crossties. She tried to avoid looking between them at the ground far below.

"Look!" Spud exclaimed.

Hildy stopped dead still on a crosstie and followed where he pointed. Ruby was about half way across the trestle. Beyond it, where the tracks vanished into a grove of oaks and pines, black smoke billowed into the air.

Hildy cupped her hands to her mouth and screamed, "Ruby, come back! A train's coming!"

Ruby stopped, glanced at the smoke, then whirled and started running back toward Hildy and Spud just as the locomotive's headlight broke out of the trees.

Hildy gasped, "She'll never make it in time!"

"Neither will we if we don't get out of here! Come on! Run! Run!"

Chapter Seventeen

DANGER AFTER DANGER

Friday Morning

Spud turned back toward the tunnel and started running along the crossties of the trestle. But Hildy was paralyzed with fear as the locomotive thundered down on her desperate cousin far out on the high span.

"Ru-by!" Hildy shrieked through her cupped hands. "Faster! Run faster!"

She saw Ruby twist her head to glance behind her. The train with its five cars was already out of the woods and onto the trestle. Hildy saw the engineer leaning out of the open cab. He rang the bell furiously. Hildy expected him to blow warning whistle blasts. Then she realized he was deliberately avoiding that, because he had no doubt been warned about noise that could start an avalanche at the tunnel.

A metallic screeching sound told Hildy that the locomotive's brakes had been applied. The iron wheels on steel rails threw showers of sparks, but the train rushed onward.

"Hildy!" Spud's shout reminded her of her own danger. "You can't help her! Come on!"

Hildy couldn't force herself to turn away. She watched fearfully as the black locomotive rapidly gained on her desperately running cousin.

Hildy's own mind screamed, *She'll never make it!*

Suddenly, Ruby seemed to trip. She lunged forward, hands outstretched.

Hildy thought of the depth of open space that ended in the dry riverbed.

Oh, no! Hildy forced her eyes shut, unable to watch any more.

For a long moment she stood still, sick beyond words at what must have happened.

Then she became aware of Spud's voice again. "Come on, Hildy! Run!" She also heard the squealing of brakes and the roar of the train as it thundered onward.

With a mighty effort of her will, and a powerful urge to survive, Hildy opened her eyes. The train hurtled closer, its momentum thrusting it onward even though the brakes were locked.

But there was no sign of Ruby.

With a broken sob, Hildy raced toward safety. Through scalding tears, she glimpsed Spud waving her on.

Hildy lost all sense of what was happening. It seemed as though she were somewhere else, watching herself run, flat out, arms and legs pumping, toward the end of the trestle. Spud was waiting, arms outstretched to grab her.

Their hands touched, then she was half pulled, half dragged off the span. As she stumbled after Spud, she felt the rumble of the train in the ties beneath her feet.

Hildy told herself, *We'll never get through the tunnel in time, and there's no place else to go!*

Spud jerked her into the mouth of the tunnel. Above the noise of the train, Hildy heard him shout, "Drop flat between the track and the wall! Get your feet under you! Pull your arms to your sides and don't move!"

Spud dove head first toward the rock wall, dragging Hildy with his right hand. Thrown off balance, she fell toward the wall between Spud and the rails. The locomotive roared into the tunnel as Hildy lay breathless in the gravel, feeling the ground tremble beneath her.

But her silent, anguished thoughts were still on her cousin. *Ruby! Oh, Ruby!*

Hildy became aware that the passing train was slowing. She cautiously raised her head. The caboose moved past and squeaked to a full stop just outside the south end of the tunnel.

Spud grabbed her hand. "Let's get out of here!"

Hildy numbly climbed to her feet and turned anguished eyes toward the high, empty trestle. There was no sign of Ruby.

With a sob, Hildy pulled away from Spud and hurried out of the tunnel. She stopped at the end of the trestle, with Spud beside her.

He warned, "Don't look!"

Hildy mumbled, "I've got to—find her." With great effort, she forced herself to look down to the dry riverbed. She held her breath, steeling herself for the terrible sight.

Confused, she murmured, "I—don't see her."

"Neither do I," Spud said.

Hildy glanced at the trestle again, which seemed to mock her by its empty silence.

Behind her, she could hear men running toward them from the train.

Hildy sagged weakly against Spud. "Oh, Ruby, Ruby!" The hot tears seeped from beneath her closed eyelids and made warm rivulets down her cheeks.

Then she felt Spud suddenly stiffen. "Hildy, look!"

She looked at him through the fog of her tears, but he wasn't looking at her. Hildy slowly turned to follow his gaze.

Over the side of the trestle they saw something move. Hildy blinked, brushed the tears from her face, and stared in disbelief.

Slowly, she made out the form of someone climbing up from the support beams to the crossties of the trestle.

"Ruby!" Hildy's scream caught in her throat. "Oh, thank God!" She began running toward her, arms outstretched.

Moments later, Ruby staggered into Hildy's embrace, dirty, scratched and cut, but alive and safe.

The next events became a blur. Hildy was only faintly aware of Skeezix, the railroader, and the four-member crew of the train hovering around them.

Hildy heard Spud urge everyone to give the cousins a moment alone.

When Hildy had stopped crying, her emotion turned to anger. She held her cousin at arm's length and scolded, "You did a terribly dumb thing!"

"I know," Ruby admitted.

"Don't you ever do that again!" Hildy cried. "Never, never!"

Ruby said a little defensively, "If'n ye'll stop a-hollerin' at me, I got a surprise fer ye."

Hildy stared at her cousin, not understanding.

Ruby motioned for Hildy and Spud to come closer, then explained, "After a-jumpin' off them tracks onto a big timber underneath, whilst I was a-scratchin' to hang on, I seen somethin'. 'Course I was so skeered o' fallin', er gittin' shook loose, I didn't pay no mind to it until after thet ol' train passed."

Hildy and Spud exchanged bewildered glances.

Ruby added, "They's some brush an' trees at the base of this here hill whar we are a-standin'. Cain't see it from here, but—"

"Ruby!" Hildy interrupted. "What did you see?"

"I seen Dixie Mae!" she said under her breath. "She's down thar."

The announcement hit Hildy with such force that she jerked her head back. "What?"

Out of earshot of the others, Ruby repeated, "I seen Dixie Mae! They's a little shack down thar, and I seen her a-standin' in front of it, a-watchin' me an' thet thar train."

Hildy felt hope surge through her. "You're absolutely sure?"

"Positive! Come on! While Ben an' Skeezix are a-talkin' to them men, I'll show y'all. I seen a path thet goes alongside this here hill." Ruby turned and started pushing past some clumps of Scotch broom.

Hildy and Spud followed, speechless.

They arrived at the bottom of the hill by following a deer path that led through small growths of manzanita, sharp buckbrush, and Scotch broom.

Hildy was breathing hard, full of excitement, hope, and fear. Ruby stopped and crouched behind a live oak. It had dense green branches that reached to the ground, providing a thick cover. Hildy and Spud crouched down beside Ruby.

Carefully easing the small, sharp-edged leaves of the oak aside, Hildy peered over Ruby's shoulder. About fifty yards ahead, a crude, one-room shack hugged the granite rock base of the mountain. The wooden structure was almost completely hidden by manzanita.

"Thar!" Ruby whispered, pointing. "See her?"

Dixie Mae Stonecipher sat on the small front porch, biting her fingernails and looking toward the trestle.

Hildy's excitement soared. She straightened up. "We've got to rescue her!" she whispered.

"Wait!" Spud's warning was almost a hiss. "She's probably being guarded."

"Maybe not," Hildy said. "She didn't try to run away with us at the barn because she knew her father expected her back. Maybe she's alone now."

"Then where's her father and the other outlaws?" Spud asked in a hoarse whisper.

"Prob'ly in them trucks an' thet Cadillac," Ruby reasoned. "Those vehicles cain't git down here. I reckon Hildy's right, an' Dixie Mae's alone."

Spud asked, "But what if Jiggs is guarding her?"

Hildy made a quick decision. "You two stay here. I'll slip up close and get her attention. Then I'll motion for her to come, and I'll lead her back here."

Spud started to protest, but Hildy wouldn't listen. She crouched low and eased herself around the spreading live oak.

A few minutes later, still breathing hard from fear and excitement, Hildy stopped again. Slowly, from the shelter of a thorny buckbrush, she raised up to where she could clearly see the outlaw's daughter.

Hildy called softly, "Dixie Mae. It's me—Hildy!"

The red-haired girl glanced around and looked surprised upon seeing Hildy.

"Come here!" Hildy urged in a whisper, motioning frantically.

Slowly, the outlaw's daughter stood and sauntered toward Hildy's hiding place. When she was within a couple of feet, Hildy whispered, "Is anybody watching you?"

"Yes," she answered softly. "Jiggs is inside. He's got a machine gun."

Hildy swallowed hard and said, "Step around this bush and follow me."

Dixie Mae stepped forward, then shook her head. "I'm scared! He's got a jug, and he's mean when he's drunk. If he sees you, he'll—"

"Don't talk!" Hildy interrupted. "Just move! Now!"

As Dixie Mae stepped around the gray buckbrush, Hildy heard a man's gruff voice call from inside the shack. "Dixie Mae, what are you doing?"

The girl stopped and looked back. "Uh—just stretching my legs."

"Well, stay where I can see you."

Dixie Mae hesitated while Hildy held her breath.

Jiggs' angry voice erupted again from the shack. "You get back in here! Now!"

Dixie Mae hung her head and started back, but Hildy's sharp voice stopped her. "If you go back, we can't help you. You've got to come now if you ever want to see your mother again!"

Dixie Mae hesitated, chewing on her nails, then took two quick steps toward Hildy.

"Crouch down and stay close to me," Hildy whispered. She grabbed Dixie Mae's hand and pulled her back up the deer trail toward Ruby and Spud.

"Dixie Mae!" The outlaw's voice sounded thick and muffled from the liquor, but with an edge of anger. "Who's that out there with you?"

Hildy threw aside all caution. Straightening up, she urged, "Come on, Dixie Mae! Run for it!"

Then Hildy heard the front door of the shack being jerked open. The outlaw's heavy boots sounded on the wooden porch as he shouted, "Hey, you girls! Stop!"

Hildy heard the unmistakable metallic *snick* of the safety being taken off the gun.

Chapter Eighteen

CAPTURED!

Friday Mid-Morning

A t the sound of the machine gun's safety being released, Hildy dove into the deer trail. "Get down!" she yelled, yanking Dixie Mae down beside her. Hildy braced herself for the burst of lead and flame from the rapid-fire weapon, but Jiggs didn't shoot.

Instead, Hildy heard Ruby let out a yell from her hiding place higher up the trail. "Hey, thar, Mister Jiggs, ye ol' outlaw! Here's a little ol' rock fer ye!"

Hildy risked taking her eyes off the narrow trail long enough to see Ruby rise from her hiding place and hurl a rock. Hildy heard it swoosh past her head and thunk solidly below. Then she heard Jiggs yell out in pain.

Ruby whooped. "I l'arned to knock squirrels outta trees back in the Ozarks, so I reckon an ol' crook like y'all's a plumb easy target. Spud, wanna try yore hand a-chonkin' rocks? Make 'im dance!"

Hildy let out a joyful shout. "Thanks, Ruby!" Then, "Come on, Dixie Mae. Now's our chance!" She grabbed the girl's hand as more rocks whistled overhead. "Climb faster," Hildy urged.

Behind her, she heard the outlaw call out. "You kids stop that—now!"

Hildy stole a glance over her shoulder. Jiggs threw up his hands to protect himself from the rocks, dodging them by jumping around on the narrow trail. He dropped his weapon in the process, and at the same moment, a small slide created by the girls' frantic climb cascaded toward the helpless man.

Trying to leap out of the way, he slipped on a patch of snow. The combination of rocks and debris caught him and knocked him off the trail.

"Yeeeowww!" Jiggs shrieked as he lost his footing, fell on his backside and started sliding down the snowy, brush-covered hill. He unsuccessfully tried to slow his descent by grabbing for Scotch broom and saplings.

Hildy stopped on the steep trail to catch her breath. "I don't think he'll bother us anymore," she told Dixie Mae. "Now, let's get you to safety."

After Hildy introduced Dixie Mae to Spud, they all scrambled up the trail toward the trestle and tunnel. As Hildy's eyes came even with the level ground of the tunnel's north entrance, she sighed with relief. They'd made it.

From behind her Spud said, "I'm surprised nobody's followed us down here to see what we were up to."

His words sent alarm bells clanging in Hildy's mind. She looked with sudden concern at Ruby, Spud, and Dixie Mae. "You don't suppose—?"

Dixie Mae gasped. She whirled to see Skeezix with his hands in the air walking ahead of several armed men.

Dixie Mae whispered, "That's my father and his gang."

Hildy instinctively ducked, trying to make herself less conspicuous, but it was too late.

"Dixie Mae!" Hux Stonecipher called. "What are you doing up here? And who are those kids with you?"

Hildy slowly stood up, studying the gang leader. He looked the same as he did when Hildy first caught a glimpse of him through the crack in the door at the old ranch house near the

Corrigan shack. Black stubble covered his narrow face. A lock of greasy dark hair fell over one eye.

Dixie Mae said calmly, "This is Hildy, and—"

"*Hildy*," Stonecipher interrupted, glaring at her. "You're the one that was going to help Dixie Mae go back to her mother. The other girl must be Ruby, then." He turned to the boy, demanding, "Who are you?"

"They call me Spud."

Stonecipher shrugged, not recognizing the name. He returned his gaze to the cousins. "Hildy and Ruby," he mused. "After Dixie Mae told me about your plan, I didn't expect you'd ever bother with her again, let alone try to help her."

Hildy said evenly, "You hit her, didn't you?"

Stonecipher looked away, avoiding his accuser's eyes. "I was suspicious about why she'd been out in the barn so long. She finally told me you were going to help her get back to her mother. Well, girls, as you can see, interfering in my business is a dumb thing to do."

"I help people when I can," Hildy replied simply.

"You made a big mistake in trying to help my daughter!" Stonecipher snapped. Suddenly he frowned. "Dixie Mae, where's Jiggs?"

"He slid down the hill. He's probably okay."

Her father turned to a skinny man with a pockmarked face standing with the other bandits. "Arch, go check on that drunken fool." Stonecipher looked back at his daughter as the man obeyed. "I'll talk to you later." He motioned to a short, balding man. "Ace, take her to the Cadillac and keep her there while I deal with these other three."

Ace nodded and took Dixie Mae's elbow. She pleaded, "Don't hurt them, Daddy!"

"Shut up!" he growled. He turned toward a heavyset man with a barrel chest. "Stumpy, you watch these kids."

The man promptly moved closer to Hildy, Ruby, and Spud.

Stonecipher continued, "Curly, Stumpy can watch this old geezer too while you—"

Skeezix sputtered, "I beg your pardon! Why, if I was a few years younger—!"

Curly, a thin-faced man with wavy locks and a scar on his forehead, jabbed the retired railroader in the ribs, breaking off his sentence.

"—find some ropes and tie them up." Stonecipher finished speaking, as though Skeezix had said nothing.

As Curly hurriedly entered the tunnel, the heavyset outlaw pushed Skeezix over to stand with Spud and the girls. Stumpy asked, "Boss, what do you want me to do with them after they're tied up?"

"I don't care, just so they're out of our way. When it's done, you—and the rest of the gang—get back here and out of sight. I want everyone ready before the gold train gets here."

Hildy, Ruby, Spud, and Skeezix were herded ahead of Stonecipher and Stumpy toward the tunnel entrance. Dixie Mae and Ace were already exiting it on the other side.

Skeezix said under his breath, "They drove up and took O'Rourke and me by surprise. O'Rourke's the railroader who warned us about a possible avalanche."

"Hey, old man!" Stonecipher growled. "Shut up!" He gave Skeezix a hard shove, making him stumble against the tunnel entrance.

Hildy whirled to face the outlaw leader, her eyes blazing. "You leave him alone!" Then she leaned down to help the retired railroader to his feet.

Stonecipher glared at her. "You got more spunk than sense, girlie."

Spud stepped toward Stonecipher. "You treat her with respect!"

Hildy looked gratefully at Spud. Helping Skeezix to stand, she asked, "Are you all right?"

He nodded as Stonecipher commanded, "Forget him! Now, move! All of you!"

The outlaws herded the captives into the semidarkness of the tunnel. Stonecipher's voice echoed. "When we're through with this job, you three kids are going to be sorry for taking sides with Dixie Mae."

"Somebody had to take her side," Hildy replied with feeling, "since her own father won't!"

"Why, you—" Stonecipher began, pulling his arm back as though to strike Hildy.

She ducked, but Spud leaped forward and grabbed the man's forearm.

"Get him off me!" Stonecipher roared.

The heavyset outlaw grabbed Spud from behind, pinning his arms to his sides. Spud struggled, but was no match for the older, more powerful man.

Hildy cried, "Stop it! Don't hurt him!" She leaped forward, trying to pry Stumpy's hands away from Spud.

"Yeah!" Ruby screeched, charging toward the leader. He stepped back in surprise and brought up his hands to defend himself as Ruby reached for his long, dark hair. It was a favorite hold Hildy had seen her cousin use many times on boys who tormented her.

Ruby yelled, "Ye on'ry ol' mud turtle! Why don't ye pick on somebody yore own age?"

Stumpy reached out and roughly pulled Ruby back before she could get her hands in the leader's hair. Ruby twisted around, trying for the same hold on Stumpy. He laughed and held her at arm's length.

"Feisty little wildcat, ain't you?" he remarked.

Stonecipher's face turned dark with anger. "Get these kids out of my sight!" he roared. "Take the old geezer over to Ace. Tell him to keep an eye on him."

Stumpy ordered all four captives to move quickly.

As they emerged from the tunnel, Hildy saw two medium-sized boulders fall across the tunnel's southern opening. One hit the rails and bounced back. The other came to rest on a tie between the rails. Hildy recalled O'Rourke's warning. With a shudder, she realized that all the angry shouting might have set off an avalanche.

She was relieved to see sunlight again. She noticed that the gasoline-powered switcher and the railcars had been moved from the spur tracks. The switcher rumbled slowly toward Hildy on the main line, pushing three boxcars, a tanker, and the old wooden passenger coach that Hildy had seen on the second spur. Two men stood in the small cab.

She recognized O'Rourke and guessed the second man was a gang member forcing him to move the cars.

Stonecipher called to a couple of other rough-looking men watching the switcher. "Get those boulders off the tracks. I want everything exactly the way we planned."

Hildy and the others stepped off the tracks as the switcher and the cars moved slowly toward the tunnel. Beyond the switcher, Hildy saw three trucks lined up beside the depot. The Cadillac was parked behind the last truck with Ace behind the wheel. Dixie Mae and Skeezix sat in the front seat beside him.

Hildy's thoughts jumped. *I wonder what's keeping Brother Ben? He should be here by now. I hope he doesn't get caught, too.*

The bandit with the scarred face emerged from the small depot with a length of rope and a pocketknife. He walked up to Spud, jerked his hands behind his back, and started to loop some rope around the boy's arms.

Stonecipher said sharply, "Not here, Curly! Don't tie them up until they're out of sight. It'll be easier that way. Hmmm— wait—I just had an idea. When Bronco stops the switcher, tie these kids up and put them in the end passenger coach. I'll have the switcher push the coach to the far end of these rail yards. That way, they'll be out of our way until we're through here."

As the switcher drew closer, Ruby asked, "Why do ye reckon they're a-movin' them ol' cars?"

Spud answered, "I think that's the way they plan to stop the gold train. The cars will be spotted when the gold train engineer sees them silhouetted against the light in the tunnel. The engineer will realize they're on the main line and stop to avoid hitting them. Then the brigands will attack."

"Smart boy," Stonecipher said. "First, we'll take care of the guards. Then we'll unload the gold onto those trucks, head for the airport, and we're off to Mexico."

The airport, of course! Hildy silently scolded herself. *I should have thought of that! They plan to truck the gold to the Quartz Hill Airport and fly it out. The police won't be expecting that! The gang could be safely in Mexico while everyone is still looking for them on the roads!*

"Boss!" Curly exclaimed under his breath. "You want them to know so much?"

"It won't matter," Stonecipher replied with a faint smile. "We'll be safely across the border before these kids can tell anyone what they know."

As the switcher came alongside pushing the cars, Stonecipher motioned to O'Rourke and the outlaw in the open cab. "Bronco, have him park that first boxcar where I originally planned. Then bring the others back, get these kids on the passenger coach, and leave them at the far end of the yards."

Bronco leaned forward, and Hildy saw that he had a heavy moustache. "Good idea, Boss! You know what's in two of those boxcars?" Without waiting for Stonecipher's reply, he said, "Dynamite!"

He pointed to O'Rourke, explaining, "He tells me that the first boxcar's empty, but the other two are loaded with cases of blasting powder. And that tanker right next to them is filled with gasoline."

Stonecipher looked up at O'Rourke, who was being forced to run the switcher. "Is that right?"

O'Rourke nodded. "This is the most hazardous kind of mixed cargo—dynamite and gasoline. They were on the siding here waiting for a clear track to go on into Quartz City. And there's something else you should know. Like I told this fellow, I haven't run one of these switchers in a long time. I don't like moving these cars, because I'm afraid I'll do something wrong and blow us all up!"

Hildy saw Stonecipher's lips twitch, showing his fear. "Be careful, but get it done as fast as you can. We're wasting time!"

As Hildy, Ruby, and Spud were forced down the tracks toward the southern end of the flat area, Hildy glanced at the Cadillac parked by the south end of the depot. Ace sat behind the wheel. Dixie Mae leaned over and stuck her head out the window. "I'm sorry," she called. "I shouldn't have told on you and Ruby, but I couldn't help—" Her sentence was cut off as Ace roughly shoved her back from the window.

Hildy nodded her understanding as Stumpy and Curly waited for the switcher to move the cars into position. When the gasoline tanker and two boxcars of dynamite gently hooked onto the ancient wooden passenger coach, Hildy, Ruby, and Spud were forced to climb onto the open rear platform. The two bandits sat the three in the last seats inside the coach, their hands bound behind their backs and their feet tied together. The outlaws left quickly without a word.

Hildy, Ruby, and Spud promptly struggled against the restraints, but the knots were secure.

Ruby stopped, puffing from exertion. "Shore wish Ben would get here! What do ye reckon's keeping him so long?"

Hildy gave up straining at the ropes on her wrists. "Even if he were, I don't know what he could do against all these men. Maybe it's better that he had some trouble—a blowout, stuck in a snowbank, or whatever. Let's see if we can untie each other."

She and Ruby turned back to back so their hands touched. Hildy began feeling for the end of the ropes on her cousin's wrists.

Hildy stopped as the coach jolted suddenly. "We're moving," she said, glancing out the window. "Mr. O'Rourke's pushing us with the switcher. Seems kind of fast."

Spud explained, "He's got to build up speed so the momentum will carry these four cars to the far end of the yard when he cuts us loose from the switcher."

A moment later, Hildy heard the sharp metallic sound of the switcher disconnecting from the cars. They rolled along rapidly, the wheels clicking as they passed over joints in the rails. Hildy could hear the switcher in the distance as it backed toward the tunnel.

Ruby mumbled with concern, "We shore are a-movin'!"

Hildy looked out the open coach door to the small observation platform with a low rail. She could see that the car was indeed moving with a good deal of speed, trailing the tanker and two boxcars behind it.

Spud said uneasily, "Looks like we could roll right on past the end of the rail yards."

Hildy glanced ahead and sucked in her breath. "Look!" she exclaimed. "The tracks are slanting down the hill!"

"We *are* going too fast!" Spud yelled, struggling again with the ropes on his wrists. "We're definitely going downhill! Unless we get off soon, we're going to be on a runaway train headed for Dead Man's Curve!"

—

Chapter Nineteen

DOWNHILL ON A RUNAWAY TRAIN

Friday Noon

Ruby snapped, "Spud, don't ye go a-sayin' sich a turr'ble thing!"

"It's true," the boy assured her. "Denying the reality of the situation is foolhardy."

"Thar ye go a-gin, spoutin' them two-dollar words!" Ruby retorted hotly.

Hildy broke in, "Stop it, both of you! We've got to get off this train, and fast! We're still not at full speed, so let's go outside and jump off while we still can."

Spud shook his head. "No! When those criminals forced us up here, you saw how high the step was from the ground! We can't jump with our hands tied behind our backs and our legs bound together."

"It cain't be no worse'n stayin' on this here ol' train till it jumps the tracks, the gasoline tanker ketches fahr, an' them dynamite cars blows up!" Ruby retorted.

"Yes, it can!" Spud said sharply. "If we jump, we'll break every bone in our bodies!"

A terrifying scream from behind echoed through the mountains. Hildy leaned against the rail and glanced back to her left. "It's Dixie Mae! She's running after us! Ace is right behind her."

Spud said solemnly, "They're too far away to catch this runaway train on foot."

As Dixie Mae let out another scream, Hildy remembered O'Rourke's warning about too much noise setting off an avalanche. She turned to Spud. "Quick! Look back on the other side and tell me where the outlaws are." Hildy watched as the boy moved with difficulty the few feet necessary to get a look back.

"They're just inside the tunnel, watching," he said.

"Good! Remember when Mr. O'Rourke warned us not to yell?" She nodded toward the towering, snow-covered peak above the tunnel. "We could cause an avalanche! Yell, scream, make all the noise you can!"

Hildy took a deep breath, threw her head back, and yelled so loud her throat hurt. Ruby followed suit, and then Spud. Far behind them, Hildy could hear Dixie Mae's fading cry as the runaway train drew farther and farther away.

After several seconds of screaming and shouting, Spud again turned to look back. At the same moment, Hildy seemed to feel the earth was shaking from something more than the increasing speed of the runaway cars. She also heard a faint rumbling that seemed to come from the heart of the mountain through which Shaw's Summit tunnel passed.

"It's happening!" Spud yelled. "Avalanche! The whole mountain's starting to slide downhill!"

"What're the outlaws doing?" Hildy asked excitedly.

Spud craned his neck to see. "They're ducking back inside the tunnel. But the entrance is being covered by the debris!"

"Good!" Hildy replied with satisfaction. "Let's hope both ends of the tunnel are closed. That'll keep most of the bandits safe for a while. They certainly can't rob the train. Now let's find a way to save ourselves."

With a rising sense of urgency, Hildy strained against the ropes binding her hands behind her back. *No use*, she thought. *They're too tight!*

Then she remembered something. "Spud, you've ridden lots of trains in your hobo days. How *do* railroad people stop cars?"

"Every railroad car has its own handbrake, so that it can be stopped and held any place the railroad people want it on the tracks." He got to his feet with difficulty and tipped his head back so his chin pointed at the coach's open rear door. "See that round iron wheel on the right side of the platform by the rail? That's it."

Hildy's eyes darted to the small outside observation area with its low guard rail. To the right, she saw the brake wheel. She hadn't noticed it before, although she had seen many like it on top of boxcars.

Spud's ankles were bound so tightly he couldn't even shuffle, so he started hopping toward the brake wheel.

Ruby protested, "Ye cain't do anythin' with yore hands tied behind yore back!"

Hildy spoke quickly. "Maybe he can! Try it, Spud!"

They all hopped out to converge around the brake wheel. Hildy stole an anxious glance down the tracks. They flashed by, vanishing under the coach as it raced downhill. Hildy gulped and turned to watch Spud.

He backed up to the brake wheel. It was rusty, flat on top, and about a foot across. It connected with a metal bar that led down to the wheels.

Hildy held her breath as Spud bent forward at the waist and raised his wrists high enough to touch the brake behind him. Only his fingers were free. They groped blindly, because he couldn't turn his head to see what he was doing.

Hildy guided him. "Up about an inch and to your right." As Spud's fingers grasped the wheel, Hildy exclaimed, "There! You've got it!"

Spud's knuckles turned white as he strained to turn the wheel. His ruddy face turned deep red. After several seconds, he stopped, puffing.

"It would be easy if I could face it and get some leverage. But with my wrists crossed, I have no strength in my arms."

"Lemme try," Ruby said grimly. "I'm as strong as any ol' boy!"

"If I can't do it," Spud snapped, "it's a cinch you can't!"

"We'll all three try," Hildy said, backing up to the wheel. "But we've got to hurry!" The brake was very cold, still crusted with a bit of snow from last night. Hildy ignored the discomfort and gripped the icy wheel. She felt Ruby's hands touch hers on the left and Spud's on the right.

"Turn to the right!" Spud said. "Together, turn!"

Hildy tried with her cousin, but both had a hard time keeping any footing on the coach's small platform. Hildy couldn't brace her legs as she normally would have on a moving train. She could only lean her lower body against the guardrail as Spud and Ruby were doing.

After a moment, Hildy panted, "It's not moving."

"It's no use," Spud announced.

Reluctantly, Hildy agreed. She let go of the wheel and straightened up. She swallowed hard, knowing that their best chance to stop the train had failed. She glanced at Ruby and Spud. Their faces showed terror and despair. Hildy dropped her fearful gaze to the sharp downhill angle of the tracks that were leading them to certain destruction.

Ruby asked in a low, hoarse voice, "How fast do ye reckon we're a'goin'?"

Hildy had no idea, but Spud guessed, "Fifty, sixty miles an hour."

"We are a-gonna die!" Ruby moaned, struggling unconsciously against the ropes.

"No, we're not!" Hildy insisted, conviction in her voice that she didn't feel in her heart. "We've got to get ourselves free. Let's go back inside and work on each other's bonds. If one of us can just get a hand free—"

Her sentence broke off as a thought flashed through her mind. *I wonder why Ben never got back from taking Jack to his school.*

She paused, stiffening as another thought struck her. "The school! If we don't get this train stopped, and it jumps the tracks at the curve, we'll crash into Twin Pines School with Jack and all the other kids in it!"

Ruby's eyes widened. "I never thought o' that!"

Hildy added grimly, "Nobody in that classroom has any idea of what's happening. It's not just our lives anymore. Quick, Ruby, scoot close to me! Let me try to untie the rope on your hands."

As Ruby hastily obeyed, Hildy glanced at Spud, speaking to him with urgency. "See if you can find something sharp that we can use to cut these ropes."

Hildy closed her eyes to better concentrate on what her fingers were doing behind her back. They were already beginning to get sore from working frantically on Ruby's hands. Hildy had found an end but couldn't get the knot loose to pull the rope through.

Oh, Lord, Hildy prayed silently, *help us, or Jack and all the other kids will be blown up with us!*

"Hurry up!" Ruby urged. "Listen to them wheels goin' lickety-split! Hurry! Hurry!"

Hildy bit her tongue, stifling a verbal protest. *I'm going as fast as I can!* she thought. She opened her eyes and asked, "You want to try mine?"

"Reckon I cain't do no worse," Ruby snapped.

Hildy felt her cousin's fingers feeling for the knot.

She's scared, Hildy told herself, *or she wouldn't speak that way to me. Well, I'm scared, too! And time's running out fast for all of us.*

Turning to look at the back of the coach, Hildy raised her voice to Spud. "Find anything?" she asked hopefully.

The boy had reached the far end of the swaying coach and started back down the center aisle. He was having a very hard time keeping his balance. "Nothing," he replied with disgust. "There's not a thing that could be used to cut these ropes."

Then, seeing the look of despair on Hildy's and Ruby's faces, he spoke in a more cheerful voice. "Even if we can't get untied and stop this runaway, we might have a chance when it derails; that is, if the dynamite isn't detonated by the impact."

"Oh?" Hildy said.

He nodded. "I once talked to a powder monkey who told me that new dynamite is rather stable. The nitro in it will stand more of a shock than when it's old. As I understand it, a boxcar load, tightly packed so there's not a lot of jarring beyond the initial one, could survive without incident."

Ruby shouted impatiently, "Speak plain! Are ye a-sayin' them two boxcars might not blow us to kingdom come after all?"

"It's possible," Spud replied. "The powder monkey said they used to set off powder by lighting the fuse with fire. Now, most dynamite is fired with a blasting cap. If those caps aren't in the same car with the dynamite, we might be okay."

Hildy scoffed, "Knowing nothing about dynamite, even I would be smart enough not to put the caps and the sticks in the same car!"

Spud nodded. "But sometimes people do." His words had an ominous tone. "Nobody expects a powder car to derail. But, of course, train wrecks do happen. If one cap is jarred enough to explode, that would detonate the others, and of course, all the dynamite."

Hildy's mouth suddenly felt dry with fear. She asked, "What about the gasoline tanker?"

"When I was hoboing, I saw one of those tankers derail. At first it was okay, except the car was ruptured at one corner and gasoline spewed out. That ran into a hobo's campfire. Naturally, the flames flashed along the trail of gas back to the tanker. I can still remember the shock waves from the explosion."

"Enough!" Hildy said sternly. "We're scared enough already." She paused, turning her head as far as she could toward Ruby. "How you doing?"

"Ain't doin' no good a-tall! This here knot shore is tight! Maybe ye better try mine ag'in."

Hildy forced her cramped fingers to grope for the knots in Ruby's ropes again. She closed her eyes. *Please, Lord!*

Opening her eyes, Hildy turned to Spud with an idea. "Can you kick out a window without getting cut?"

The boy shot her a confident look. "These calf-length boots should protect me." He sprawled into a seat and raised his bound feet. "Just one second!"

Hildy couldn't look any longer. She turned her head until she heard breaking glass. She glanced anxiously toward Spud as he swung his booted feet down and sat up.

"Got it!" Spud's voice was triumphant. "And I didn't get cut."

Hildy could see that most of the glass had fallen to where it would be hard for Spud to pick it up. But two sharp pieces still remained intact.

Spud stood up and backed carefully toward the broken window. "If I can find that shard without cutting my wrists—ouch!"

"Are you cut?" Hildy asked, her fingers momentarily still.

"I can't see my hands. I'm not sure."

"I'll come help," Hildy said.

She hopped down the aisle to examine his wrists. "It's your thumb, but it's not cut deep," she assured him. "Try it again. Careful!"

With Hildy guiding Spud in what direction to move his hands, he eased the ropes across the shard imbedded in the windowsill. "Now," Hildy said, hope rising, "gently move your wrists up and down. Slowly! Slowly!"

Spud did as she said, his jaw muscles twitching with the tension. He said evenly, "If this doesn't work, and we don't stop this train in time, there's no way the authorities will recognize our remains and realize a crime has been committed. They'll probably calculate that we fooled around with the brakes and caused the runaway."

"We're *going to make it*," Hildy said firmly, watching the shard of glass slowly slice through the ropes.

"There!" she exclaimed triumphantly as the rope fell from Spud's wrists. "Thank you, Lord!" she whispered.

Seconds later, their hands and feet free, the three made a mad dash for the observation platform. Hildy's heart sped up as she saw how fast they plunged into a short tunnel.

"Quick!" she cried, grabbing the brake wheel. "Help me! We've got to get this thing stopped in time!"

Ruby joined her cousin and Spud in straining to turn the stubborn brake wheel. Hildy held her breath, throwing her weight behind the effort. Suddenly, the wheel gave a little.

"It's turning!" she shouted in triumph. "It's turning!"

Hildy felt tears of joy burst forth as she took another grip. The brake wheel turned easier, faster, and the brakes began to take hold. The swaying coach shuddered as the locked wheels squealed on the rails. The brake wheel stopped turning.

Spud explained, "That's as tight as it goes. Let's hope the car stops in time."

The runaway train screeched out of the tunnel into a narrow rock canyon heavily forested with ponderosas. The old wooden coach trembled violently, swaying from side to side, as if it would jump the tracks, but the cars plunged on.

Spud said anxiously, "All that friction's going to start a fire, maybe in the journal boxes."

Ruby said in a hoarse, cracked voice, "We ain't a-gonna slow up enough! We're a-goin' into the curve! An' lookee yonder!"

Hildy's eyes followed Ruby's pointing arm. "The school!" she gasped. "We're coming up on it!"

Spud added, "We're slowing, but it'll never stop in time! We're going to derail on the curve. Quick! Get over to the uphill side and get ready to jump as it leaves the tracks!"

Moments later, Hildy felt the coach lunge as it went into the sharp curve. She grabbed for the rail just as the end of the car rose into the air. She felt the coach roll from under her feet.

"It's going over!" she yelled. "Jump!" She leaped away from the moving car.

Then she was flying through the air filled with the sound of the tanker and boxcars leaving the tracks.

Hildy heard the crumpling of metal and crushing of wood, and steeled herself for the last sound she might ever hear—a fiery explosion.

CHAPTER
TWENTY

OUT OF THE
WRECKAGE

Friday Afternoon

Hildy had sailed through the air perilously close to the gasoline tanker that followed the coach off the tracks. *Lord, don't let them come down on top of me!* she prayed.

In the few seconds she was airborne, Hildy glimpsed the ancient wooden passenger coach from which she had jumped as it rolled onto its side with a sickening, crunching sound. Snow and mud shot through the air like dirty globs of rain. The front and back wheels of the coach were violently torn off and tossed precariously into the air. Flames shot up from the journal box, and the coach was crushed as the gasoline-laden tanker plowed into it from behind.

The violent collision of splintering wood and screeching metal sounded almost like a woman screaming in pain. As the gasoline car hit the coach, Hildy saw it burst into splinters of wooden shrapnel.

The weight of the gasoline, shifting to the lower end, forced the tanker's front end to turn sharply upward. The tanker's rusty iron wheels and carriage assembly dangled like the front legs of some grotesque beast over the broken remains of the coach.

Gasoline spouted from a rupture in the tanker's midsection, trailing downhill toward the burning journal box. The two cars of dynamite still stood upright, swaying unsteadily from where they'd broken free of the tanker. The boxcars plowed up the soft ground, throwing snow and mud aside as they slid behind the demolished coach.

It's all going to blow up! The thought jarred Hildy's brain. She'd landed so hard beside the tracks that countless little white specks danced before her eyes like miniature exploding stars. She felt sharp pain throughout her body, then everything went black.

As though from a great distance, she heard Spud calling her name. Her eyes popped open as Spud knelt beside her. His face was covered with gravel and mud.

He spoke urgently, "We've got to get away from here before everything blows up!"

Dazed, not remembering what had happened, Hildy felt Spud pulling on her hands, and she glimpsed the blurred wreckage of the train. The shock of it cleared her mind.

Black smoke churned up from the burning journal box. The silver rivulet of gasoline from the ruptured tanker continued to flow toward the flames.

Hildy asked weakly, "Where's Ruby?"

"Over there." Spud jerked his head to the left.

Hildy managed to turn her head. She saw Ruby lying face down and motionless in a snowbank.

"We've got to help her!" Hildy urged. She swayed unsteadily to her feet. "I can walk."

Spud took her arm as they moved haltingly toward her cousin. Hildy cringed, half-expecting a tremendous explosion any minute. *If that blows while we're this close—* She shook the thought from her mind.

Kneeling beside Ruby, Hildy begged, "Speak to me!" She turned her cousin's face toward her. It was bruised and lacerated, and bits of gravel stuck to the cuts. Her eyes were open but unfocused.

"Can you walk?" Hildy asked anxiously. "We've got to get away from here! That whole train's going to blow up! Spud, grab her arm. I'll take the other one."

Hildy's anxious words seemed to penetrate Ruby's dazed mind. She straightened abruptly and stared at the tangled mass of what had been the passenger coach, and the rising column of smoke and fire from the journal box.

Ruby lurched to her feet. "Shore I kin walk! Fact is, I kin run. Now, either run with me, er git outta muh way."

As Hildy, Ruby, and Spud half-ran, half-staggered across the open flat field away from the wreckage, Hildy could hear the excited voices of children. She glanced toward Twin Pines School and saw students huddled at the windows. A few were running out of the building, Jack Tremayne among them. He was followed by the teacher.

"Jack, get back!" Hildy screamed. "Fire! Dynamite! Gasoline! Go back!"

Spud raised his voice. "Jack, tell the teacher to get all the kids away from here! That train's going to blow up any minute!"

Hildy was relieved to see Jack speak to the woman. Then the two began herding the students away from the school and down the muddy road.

Hildy stole a fearful glance back at the wreck. A whirling column of black smoke leaped into the air from the back end of what remained of the coach. Hungry yellow flames licked tentatively at the gasoline tanker.

"Faster!" Hildy yelled, turning away from the fearful sight. "Faster!"

Hildy's breath was coming in ragged gasps as the three raced side by side to the barbed-wire fence that ran along the rutted road, covered now with mud and melting snow. She felt her back muscles tighten as she cringed in anticipation of the blast that could take their lives in a matter of seconds.

"There's a ditch just beyond that fence!" she blurted, panting hard and fighting for breath. "If we can get to it, we'll be safe."

As the trio came nearer the three-strand fence, Hildy noticed that a car had slid into the ditch, stopping at a strange angle. "It's Brother Ben's Packard!" she exclaimed. "That's why he didn't come back! He must have—"

"Stop yore jabberin'!" Ruby interrupted. "Jist git through this fence an' into that ol' ditch."

Spud placed his left foot on the lower strand of wire and gingerly lifted the middle wire so the girls could get through. When both were on the other side, they held the wires apart for him.

Hildy slid into the ditch in front of the Packard. She was relieved to see that the old ranger wasn't in the car. "He must have gotten a ride back up."

The others followed Hildy into the wet slush at the bottom of the ditch. There was a flash across the sky as Hildy shouted, "Down!" She instinctively pulled Ruby and Spud face down into the mud just as an explosion shook the ground beneath them. Another blast followed so close Hildy thought they were one.

Spud yelled, "The fire finally reached the gasoline tanker and set it off. The concussion set off the dynamite. Cover your head with your hands! Debris will be falling any second."

Hildy cringed in the ditch, closing her eyes and covering her ears and head with her arms. She could feel the debris raining down around them. She forced back the thought of larger chunks falling on top of them.

Other thoughts flashed through Hildy's mind so rapidly she couldn't focus on any one of them. *Dixie Mae. Her outlaw father and the others trapped in the tunnel. Brother Ben. Joey—.*

Her thoughts slowed as she realized the debris had stopped falling. Hildy heard the roar of flames as they consumed the wooden coach. She glanced at Ruby and Spud and uttered a grateful sob that they were safe beside her.

Slowly, cautiously, Hildy raised her head to join Spud and Ruby in peering over the top of the ditch toward the wreck.

"Lookee thar!" Ruby whispered in awe. "Ain't nothin' left of that ol' train. Jist a great big burnin' hole in the ground."

"The schoolhouse is gone," Spud said quietly. "But it looks like the kids and their teacher are safe."

Hildy looked away from the burning hole. Scattered pieces of the wreckage burned over a wide area. She glanced at the foundations of the school and tankhouse. Beyond them, down the muddy road, she could seen children milling about, apparently none the worse for their close call.

Then Hildy heard the sound of sirens in the distance. An ancient red fire engine wailed toward the scene, followed by a string of cars. *The explosion must have been heard for miles around*, Hildy thought. *Someone called the volunteer fire department.*

Hildy rose slowly to her feet beside Ben's car. "Jack will know for sure if Brother Ben got a ride back to the tunnel. If he did, he was probably worried sick when he heard about our being trapped on that runaway train. Maybe we can get one of the firemen to give us a ride back to the tunnel."

Spud nodded. "Right. There's no sense sticking around here. Let's see if someone will give us a lift."

The three ran to where Jack and the teacher stood and told them about what had happened. Jack confirmed that Ben's car had slid into the ditch because of the snow and ice. The old ranger had been so anxious to get back to Hildy and her friends at the tunnel that he had borrowed the teacher's car.

Hildy told of their urgent need to get back to the tunnel to find Dixie Mae, and the teacher asked a volunteer fireman to take them. He was still wearing his green grocer's apron when Hildy, Ruby, and Spud piled into his boxy old Nash and headed back to Shaw's Summit.

As the car wound up the narrow rural road, Hildy noticed for the first time that her hands were bleeding. Her clothes were torn and mud-stained. She looked at Spud and Ruby and realized they were not in any better shape. They both had cuts and bruises. *Thank the Lord we're all alive*, Hildy thought.

Aloud, she said, "All my concerns about Joey and Dixie Mae tumbled through my mind while we were in the ditch. I wondered why Brother Ben hadn't returned, and if Dixie Mae would ever get home safely to her mother. The only thing I felt good about was the fact that Hux Stonecipher and his gang were trapped in the tunnel. Then I thought about little Joey, and wondered if he had that ear surgery. And if he did, how would my daddy pay for it?"

Spud tried to encourage her. "I'm sure there will be money available when your brother needs that operation."

Hildy gave Spud a grateful smile. "I think so, too, but I don't know how. As I told Dixie Mae, all things are possible to those who believe. But back in that ditch I thought, 'I'll never grow up to be a teacher; we'll never get our *forever* home.'

"Then I scolded myself, because I believe everyone is born for a purpose, and I hadn't finished the work I felt God had called me to do. I knew then we were all going to make it."

The driver announced, "Shaw's Summit is just around the next curve."

Hildy eagerly leaned forward. She sucked in her breath as the scene came into view. "It's gone!" she whispered in awe. "The mountain top's disappeared."

"An' so's the tunnel!" Ruby added. "They ain't nothin' left but them thar little ol' tracks!"

It was true. The avalanche had torn away the top half of the peak, plunging snow and rock down to bury the railroad tunnel. Only the narrow-gauge rails of the main line led away from an immense mass of boulders, snow, brush and dirt. The gasoline switcher and one boxcar lay on their side where the avalanche had swept them. Several railroad men scurried around the area.

Spud observed, "Those men must be from the gold train. It's got to be just out of sight behind that mound of dirt."

"There's Brother Ben and Mr. O'Rourke!" Hildy exclaimed, pointing. "But where's Dixie Mae?"

"An' Skeezix," Ruby added. "Whar's he at?"

"The Cadillac's gone, but the outlaws' three trucks are still here," Spud said. "I'll bet the outlaws that weren't trapped in the tunnel escaped in the car. I sure hope they didn't take Dixie Mae as a hostage."

"Me too!" Hildy said with feeling as the volunteer fireman pulled off the road and onto the shoulder near the depot. Hildy hurried out of the car, thanking the driver as she raced with Ruby and Spud toward the old ranger and O'Rourke.

Ben threw his arms around all three and held them close. "I'm sure glad to see all of you!" he said huskily. "I've been frantic ever since Mr. O'Rourke told me you were on that runaway train. How did you ever live through it?"

"We'll tell you later," Hildy said. "Where's Dixie Mae?"

O'Rourke motioned toward the depot. "She's inside with Skeezix. I've got to phone the superintendent that you're alive!"

Hildy hurried after O'Rourke, followed by Ben, Ruby, and Spud. As Hildy left the bright outdoors to enter the gloomy, old-smelling depot, she could barely make out two people sitting on an old wooden bench. "Is that you, Dixie Mae?" she asked.

The red-haired girl jumped up. "Hildy!" She threw her arms around her. "I thought you'd all been killed on that runaway train!"

"It was a close call," Hildy admitted, taking the girl's hands in hers. "But are you all right?"

"Oh, yes!" Dixie Mae exclaimed happily. "Thanks to you and your friends."

Hildy looked at Skeezix. "How about you?"

"Haven't had this much excitement since I retired," the old railroader assured her with a big grin.

Dixie Mae pointed to O'Rourke, who sat at a desk with earphones on his head, speaking into an upright telephone. "He's going to call my mother as soon as the railroad company's private line is free. It's been busy ever since the avalanche. First they had to send word to stop the gold train before it reached the tunnel."

"It's closed on both sides," Skeezix explained. "The outlaws have just enough air to survive until the rescue team gets here."

"Then," Dixie Mae continued as though Skeezix hadn't spoken, "Mr. O'Rourke called the sheriff's office and told them to be on the lookout for the Cadillac with Ace and the others, who weren't trapped in the tunnel."

Ben commented in his slow drawl, "They won't get far. Meantime, those in the tunnel aren't going anyplace, except to prison after they're rescued."

Hildy suddenly thought of Dixie Mae's father. "Is your dad in the tunnel?"

Absently nibbling on a fingernail, she answered, "Yes."

Hildy said gently, "He'll go to jail, you know. How do you feel about that?"

Before she could answer, O'Rourke turned from the phone. "Hildy," he said, his face somber, "I have the railroad superintendent on the line. He wants to talk to you."

O'Rourke stood up, removed the earphones from his head, handed them to Hildy, and told her to sit down.

Hildy placed the strange receivers over her ears, sat on the edge of the chair, and leaned toward the mouthpiece of the phone. "Hello, this is Hildy Corrigan."

A man's gruff voice came over the wire. "Your father wants you to come home right away. Your brother's had another seizure and has to have an operation at once."

Chapter Twenty-one

THE NEWS AT HOME

Afterward

Hildy was numb with concern about her little brother as she said goodbye to O'Rourke and Skeezix. Then she followed Ben to the teacher's borrowed Hudson sedan. Hildy sat in back between Ruby and Dixie Mae. Spud rode up front with the old ranger. As the car headed downhill toward what had been Twin Pines School, Hildy closed her eyes and prayed silently for Joey.

She also asked the Lord to help her father find a way to pay for the ear surgery. She wasn't aware her lips were moving until Ruby leaned over to her.

"Don't ye fret none. He's a-gonna be fine."

Hildy opened her eyes as Dixie Mae added, "Remember what you told me in the barn about all things working for good to those who believe? Well, it worked out for me just as you said."

"Thanks," Hildy replied, managing to smile at both girls. "I'll feel better when I'm at Joey's side."

The old ranger looked in the rearview mirror and said, "It'll be several hours before we're back in Lone River, Hildy. Joey will be through the surgery by that time. I'm sorry we can't get there sooner, but believe me, he's going to be all right."

"I think so, too, Brother Ben, but I'm concerned for my daddy, too. He must be worried sick, knowing there's no money to pay for the operation."

"I wasn't going to say anything yet," the old ranger replied, "but O'Rourke told me that the railroad superintendent was very grateful for the way you kids trapped those outlaws and prevented the gold-train robbery. O'Rourke was sure there'd be a reward."

"A reward?" Hildy asked in surprise.

"Yup!" Ben smiled. "Part of it will be yours, Hildy. I suspect there will be enough money to help your father pay Joey's doctor bills."

Hildy smiled, too, aware that one more thing was working out the way she'd believed, although she never dreamed *how* it would happen.

When they reached the site of the derailment, Hildy chafed at the delay caused by the sheriff's deputies who insisted on asking questions about the runaway train. Hildy, Ruby, and Spud each gave their statements while the old ranger paid a nearby rancher to pull the Packard from the ditch with his team of mules.

When the questions were finally over, they all said goodbye to Jack. Noticing a lingering look between him and Ruby, Hildy turned with Spud and Dixie Mae to look at the blackened, twisted devastation of what had once been four runaway railroad cars and a one-room country schoolhouse.

Then, with a silent prayer of gratitude that nobody had been badly hurt, Hildy slid into the mud-splattered Packard along with the others. The old ranger headed toward the San Joaquin Valley.

In spite of her concern about Joey, Hildy managed to eat one of the sandwiches that ranchers' wives had sent to the volunteer firemen. When she finished eating, she turned and smiled at Dixie Mae. "Do you realize you haven't bitten your fingernails since we got into this car?"

The red-haired girl seemed surprised. "Maybe it's because I've had so much to think about. I never knew anybody could care so much about a stranger like me—you kids risked your lives to help me. I've learned something that I'll never forget." She blinked back the sudden tears and said softly and fervently, "Thank you all!"

Hildy patted Dixie Mae's hand. "You were worth it." She added, "Back there at the depot, I asked how you felt about your father going to jail, but you didn't answer me."

"Oh," Dixie Mae sniffed and managed a smile to cover her deep emotions. "Sort of mixed-up, I guess. I'm sad, because he's my father. But in another way I'm glad, because now I can go home to my mother. I always felt embarrassed being an outlaw's daughter. It wasn't so bad when Mom and I moved to where nobody knew us, but after what just happened gets in all the papers, everybody will know who I am, and that will hurt."

Ben commented, "Maybe you're looking at it the wrong way, Dixie Mae. You're not responsible for your father's actions, only your own."

Hildy agreed. "Eventually we all have to come to terms with what we can and can't change. You can't change your father, but because you're a good person, nothing your father says or does can affect you unless you allow it to."

Spud added, "You may never be entirely free of the stigma of being an outlaw's daughter. It's something you'll have to learn to live with. But the way you look at things can make a difference as to how much you suffer personally."

Ruby said, "Reckon I don't understand that two-dollar word, *stigma*, but I think I know what Spud means. It's yore choice, Dixie Mae."

For a moment the girl frowned as though in deep thought, then she brightened. "I believe you're all right! I'm not responsible for my father's choices, only my own. I choose to be me—Dixie Mae Stonecipher, a nice person."

"Good for you!" Hildy exclaimed, giving Dixie Mae a quick hug.

It was late afternoon when Ben slowed the big Packard at Lone River. Hildy leaned forward in the backseat as Ben parked in front of the small clinic that served the town. There was no hospital.

Hildy jumped out of the Packard and hurried to the door. She blinked as her eyes adjusted from the sunlight to the dimly lit waiting room. Men, women, and children stared at her from their seats along the walls.

Hildy's father rose from a chair near the open door that led down a long hallway. His eyes were bloodshot and he looked weary, but he managed a smile as he hugged his oldest daughter.

Hildy quickly kissed him on the cheek, then asked anxiously, "How's Joey?"

"Come see for yourself," he replied. Joe took her hand and led her down the hallway while the others sat down to wait.

Hildy wasn't sure what to expect as her father opened the door to a small room and motioned for her to enter. Fearfully, Hildy stepped inside.

The shade on the window was raised, and the late afternoon sunlight streamed in. Molly stood beside a small white crib with the sides raised. Hildy glimpsed the small, still form of her baby brother through the slats. Her heart skipped a beat.

Molly whispered, "He's asleep, but he came through the surgery without any problem. He's going to be fine."

Thank you, Lord! Hildy gave her stepmother a firm hug and glanced down at Joey. His blue eyes blinked open.

"Hi!" Hildy said softly, leaning over the crib. A white gauze bandage was wrapped around his head, covering his ears.

A big grin spread across Joey's face as he lifted his hands to his sister. Hildy's eyes misted with sudden tears. She reached down to take a small hand in hers.

———

That evening Joey was allowed to leave the hospital. Because the Corrigan's tar-paper shack had been made unlivable by the outlaws, the family and Dixie Mae stayed at Ben Strong's home that night.

Early the next morning, Hildy happily joined Ruby and Spud as the old ranger drove Dixie Mae to San Francisco. There they put her on a commercial airliner for the last leg of her journey back to her mother.

Sunday morning Hildy and her family, together with Joey, attended the small church where Ruby's father was to deliver his first sermon as the regular pastor.

Hildy slipped into the wooden pew and closed her eyes in a moment of silent prayer. All their goals had been achieved. Joey was recovering, the gold-train robbery had been thwarted and the bandits apprehended, and Dixie Mae was being reunited with her mother.

The railroad superintendent had phoned Ben's house early that morning confirming that the grateful company not only had a cash reward for Hildy, Spud, and Ruby, but would also pay Joey's doctor bill. And just before they left for church, a telegram had arrived saying that Dixie Mae was safely home with her mother.

In spite of feeling good about all that had happened, Hildy saw new problems arising. Their tar-paper shack had been so badly vandalized that the Corrigan family would have to move again. Hildy hated the thought of that, but she refused to forsake her dream of someday having a "forever" home.

Hildy's father had been laid off work, and he didn't know when he'd be called back, if ever.

Christmas was less than a month away. It would be the Corrigan family's first in California, and they still faced the same hard times that continued to grip the whole nation.

Still, Hildy felt good. The final line of the telegram from Dixie Mae's mother echoed pleasantly in her mind: "Dixie Mae says she'll never forget that all things are possible to those who believe."

Hildy nodded to herself. It was a reassuring promise with which to face the future.